Robert Brown

Poseidon

Robert Brown

Poseidon

ISBN/EAN: 9783337385491

Printed in Europe, USA, Canada, Australia, Japan

Cover: Foto ©Andreas Hilbeck / pixelio.de

More available books at **www.hansebooks.com**

POSEIDÔN:

LINK BETWEEN SEMITE, HAMITE, AND ARYAN.

BEING

AN ATTEMPT TO TRACE THE CULTUS OF THE GOD TO
ITS SOURCES, WITH ILLUSTRATIONS OF THE HISTORY OF
THE KYKLÔPES, HYKSOS, PHŒNICIANS, AITHIOPES
OR CUSHITES, AND PHILISTINES.

BY ROBERT BROWN, JUN. F.S.A.

'Poseidôn, sire of gods and men.'
Orphic Hymn.

CONTENTS.

POSEIDÔN.

SECTION I.

IMPERFECT SUPREMACY OF THE HOMERIC ZEUS.

In the following pages I shall attempt to trace the origin of the conception of the great Homeric and Hellenic deity Poseidôn, and, in so doing, to illustrate his remarkable position in the mythology of the Greeks. The subject is necessarily obscure and replete with difficulty; for although so much has been written respecting the belief and religious systems of the Ancients, yet modern discovery is ever supplying fresh material for investigation, and frequently disproving long-cherished theories and ideas. Religious Mythology, and the mist-wrapped history of the Earlier Time, will always have a certain peculiar fascination; and

B

I trust that minds susceptible of it may find the
present enquiry neither uninteresting nor unin-
structive.   That the principal point which I wish
to establish may be clearly understood, I here
lay down the following proposition : *Poseidôn,
in origin, is not an Aryan, but a Semitic and
Hamitic' divinity, and his cultus passed over
into Greece from Chaldaea by way of Phoenicia
and Libyê.*   This I shall attempt to demonstrate,
and with what success the reader must judge.

The Hellénes, as the descendants of Javan,
were Japhetites, and of the Indo-Germanic or
Aryan family of nations.   In Scripture they are
called ' the sons of the Javanites,' [1] and their established religion and mythology were, therefore,
Aryan, and, as such, were similar in origin with
the creed and cultus of Persian and Hindu in
the East, and Latin, Celt, and Teuton in the
West.   But though such was the character of the
national faith, yet the early intercourse between
Greece and the eastern shores of the Mediterranean resulted in the introduction of the element
of nonconformity through Semitic and Hamitic
channels, which element, although in a very decided minority, was nevertheless both active and

[1] Joel iii. 6.

powerful. Thus the clashing of creeds and their opposing supporters on earth reacted on the regions of Olympos, and produced a prolonged Theomachy, or contest of the Gods. In Zeus, the great Aryan divinity, we observe two distinct phases: (1) An embodiment of human conceptions of the one God, and (2) The most extended powers of deity that could be imagined supplied by man with his own appetites and passions. The worshipper coloured his divinity from mortal copies, and yet could not entirely deprive himself of some sense of the true greatness and holiness of God : hence the curious dual character of Zeus.[1] At the time of the Trojan war the Aryan Overlord had emerged triumphant from a tremendous struggle. He had defeated and crushed his sire and his sire's adherents, not, however, unaided, but by the assistance of powerful allies ;[2] and even since his conquest over Kronos and the Titânes, his sway had been endangered, notably by the attempt of Poseidôn, Hêrê, and Athênê to bind him, which it seems would actually have succeeded but for the intervention of the

[1] Cf. Rev. G. W. Cox, Mythology of the Aryan Nations, i. 4.
[2] Hes. Theog. 630–731.

Ouranid Briareôs.[1] Zeus, then, as we see him
in Homer, was the head though not the source
of deities; but his pre-eminence was the result
of conquest, and was far from being absolute and
undisputed. Ôkeanos, for instance, though not
the head, was *a* source of deities,[2] a trace, according to Sir J. Lubbock,[3] of an earlier stage of
religious development, when Water-worship may
have prevailed;[4] and when Themis is sent to
summon all divinities to a general council, although he appears to have been summoned, yet
he did not come,[5] 'Because,' says Mr. Gladstone,
'he could not appear there in his proper place as
head and sire of all.'[6] Ôkeanos, then, was far
from formally acknowledging the supremacy of
Zeus, which was even openly derided by the
Kyklôps Polyphêmos, who says scornfully to
Odysseus, 'We Kyklôpes care not for aigis-bearing
Zeus, nor the blessed gods, since we are much
mightier than they.'[7]

[1] Il. i. 406.   [2] Il. xiv. 201.
[3] Origin of Civilization, 199.   [4] Cf. Pindar. Olymp. i. 1.
[5] Il. xx. 7.   [6] Juv. Mun. 345.
                 [7] Od. ix. 276.   .

SECTION II.

POSIDÔNIC THEORY OF THE REV. G. W. COX.

But the true Homeric rival of Zeus is Poseidôn, who, although to some extent his inferior and even his vassal, is, nevertheless, much such a vassal as was Richard I. to the Crown of France; and I think that a careful examination of his character, attributes, and position, will not fail to demonstrate that he is undoubtedly the most conspicuous and remarkable of the Homeric foreign or non-Aryan members of the Hellenic theogony. It will be desirable, however, in the first place, to consider an attempt which has been made to transform the Lord of the Sea into an Aryan divinity; and for this purpose I must refer to the theory of the Rev. G. W. Cox, as expressed in his truly great work 'The Mythology of the Aryan Nations,' in which, with perhaps some very slight exceptions, he treats all Hellenic deities as if they were purely Aryan, and appears to ignore the Semitic and Hamitic elements in the Greek Pantheon. With respect to the meaning of the name Poseidôn, Mr. Cox seems to

have long doubted. In his 'Manual of Mythology' we find: *Question* '(56). What is the
meaning of the name Poseidón? *Ans.* It is not
known with certainty.'[1] But in the 'Mythology
of the Aryan Nations' he has returned to the
old attempted derivation which connected the
name with such words as potos, posis, and potamos, referring to which Gale, writing about 1670,
observes, 'Grammarians in vain attempt to
deduce the name Poseidón from the Greek tongue,
seeing, as Herodotus in *Euterpe* assures us, the
name was at first used by none but the Libyans
or Africans, who alwaies honored this god.'[2] In
vain Preller, whom Mr. Cox quotes, chases various
forms of the word through the Greek dialects.
Poseidón and potamos each begin with the same
syllable, but that is all they have in common, as
probably most unbiassed minds will readily conclude. But the reason of the wish to connect
the god's name with water, rain, or liquid in some
form, is soon apparent. Although Mr. Cox's
aërial regions are already crowded with Aryan
divinities, yet still there is room ; and so even
the terrestrial, not to say chthonian, Poseidón,

---

[1] Second edit. 17.   [2] Court of the Gentiles, ii. 6.

must with great difficulty, for the Earth-shaker is broad-breasted,[1] be hoisted up on high to re-appear as Zeus Ombrios, Jupiter Pluvius, King of the Showers. His territorial disputes, of which more anon,[2] according to Mr. Cox, 'mark simply the process which gradually converted Poseidôn the lord of the rain-giving atmosphere into the local king of the sea. It is the degradation of Zeus Ombrios to the lordship of a small portion of his ancient realm.'[3]

But, ere we thus degrade Poseidôn, let us have some proof that he ever was an air-god. The place is so well filled by 'cloud-compelling Jove,' that the strongest evidence should be advanced in his favour ere Poseidôn can be allowed to share the Thunderer's especial realm. But Mr. Cox thinks that the 'earlier identity of Poseidôn with his brother is attested by the name Zenoposeidon.' To what remote period are we to go back in search of this earlier identity? The sphere, character, and power of the Lord of Aigai are most clearly exhibited, and very fully illustrated, in the Homeric poems; but there is not the faintest suggestion of any identity between him and Zeus.

[1] Il. ii. 478.   [2] Vide Sec. XXI.
[3] Mythology of the Aryan Nations, ii. 264.

But is the application of the name Zeus to Poseidôn, in traditions ‘ later and extraneous ’[1] or even in traditions of equal antiquity with the Iliad and the Odyssey, in itself any proof of the identity of the two divinities? The name is given alike to all the three Kronid brothers: Aïdês is called both by Homer[2] and Hesiod,[3] Zeus Chthonios, Zeus of the Underworld. Homer never calls Poseidôn the Zeus of the sea; but the meaning is perfectly clear; *i.e.* that, in their respective spheres, Aïdês and Poseidôn were sovereign rulers, and so corresponded in some degree to the great head of all, the supreme Zeus himself. A lady may well be described as being the queen of her household, without being thereby identified with the Sovereign. But perhaps it may be contended that Aïdês, because styled the Zeus of the Underworld, is therefore identical with Zeus the Highest; and that, in fact, the three Kronid brothers in reality represent but one person, Zeus, God. Such treatment of a mythology would render its analysis an impossibility. The Kronid brothers being represented as separate personages, we must treat them as such, and investigate their

---

[1] Juv. Mun. 248.   [2] Il. ix. 457.   [3] Erg. kai. Hêm. 468.

several antecedents. Infinitely difficult as it is to raise Poseidôn to the heavens, and convert him into an aërial deity, it would be far more so, nay, utterly impossible, to elevate the King of Erebos himself, and to identify him with Zeus, Lord of the pure Aithêr. Even to bring up his dog to earth, not heaven, formed the crowning labour of Hêraklês. We may then, I think, safely conclude that the epithet Zênoposeidôn does not necessarily identify the two elder sons of Kronos.

SECTION III.

SUGGESTIONS AS TO THE MEANING OF THE NAME POSEIDÔN.

PLATÔN makes a guess at the meaning of the name Poseidôn, which, however incorrect, is to some extent ingenious. He derives it παρά τὸ πόσιν δοῦναι, from his giving drink, ' i.e. the sea and water unto al,' explains Gale,[1] who has

---

[1] Court of the Gentiles, ii. 6.

assumed that Poseidôn is identical with Neptune,
and is endeavouring to identify both with Japhet.
This conjecture of Platôn would suit Mr. Cox's
Posidônic Zeus Ombrios very well; but as that
mysterious divinity had disappeared from Hellenic
mythology long before the time of Homer, Platôn
would necessarily know nothing about him, and
therefore probably intended his derivation to be
understood in the manner suggested by Gale.
But a moment's reflection shows the absurdity
of such an interpretation of the name, for 'posis'
is essentially something to drink—the thing which
of all others the sea does not supply.   However, a
conclusive reason for rejecting a watery derivation
of Poseidôn's name is the fact, so well observed
by Mr. Gladstone, and which, I think, is fully
apparent on investigation of the matter, that
'though god of the sea, he is not, so to speak, the
sea-god, or the water-god.   He has in him nothing
of an elemental deity.   He is not placed in as
near a relation to water as Zeus is to air, by the
epithet Diïpetes, and the phrase Dios ombros.
These very phrases show us that he was not, in
Homer's view, the god of moisture, or even of
water, generally.   The attempts to derive his

name from a common root with "posis" drink, or
" potamos " a river, would therefore be insufficient
or inappropriate, even if they were not, as they are,
somewhat equivocal.' [1]

SECTION IV.

MR. COX'S TREATMENT OF THE CONNECTION BETWEEN POSEIDÔN AND THE HORSE.

I SHALL next notice Mr. Cox's treatment of the
remarkable connection between Poseidôn and
the Horse. He says, ' That Poseidôn should
become the lord and tamer of the horse was a
necessary result (!) as soon as his empire was
definitely limited to the sea. As the rays of the
sun become the Harits and Rohits, his gleaming
steeds, so the curling waves with the white crests
would be the flowing-maned horses of the sea
king.' [2] Mr. Ruskin, in his delightful ' Queen of
the Air,' speaks still more positively to the
same effect. He says of Poseidôn, ' Neptune
over the waters, and the flow and force of life—

[1] Juv. Mun. 243.
[2] Mythology of the Aryan Nations, ii. 263.

always among the Greeks typified by the horse,
which was to them as a crested sea wave ani-
mated and bridled.'[1] The first proposition here
laid down is, that there is a peculiar abstract
connection between the horse and the sea : therefore Poseidôn, being the sea god, necessarily
became the horse god. But Mr. Cox himself, by
reminding us of the horses of the sun,[2] at once
disproves the truth of such an idea. Indra and
Apollôn are not sea gods, yet have they chariots
and horses; and it would be just as reasonable
to assert, conversely, that there is a peculiar
abstract connection between the sky or the sun
and the horse. The truth seems to be, that
Poseidôn being found to be connected both with
the sea and the horse, it was thought necessary
to suggest a link between these two; then fancy
stepped in, and compared the waves to horses;
and although it is somewhat difficult to entirely
disprove unsupported assertions of this kind, yet
we may do so by illustrating, on the one hand,
their inherent weakness, and supplying, on the
other, a more probable explanation. We have
observed that there is no peculiar abstract con-

---

[1] Queen of the Air, i. 13.   [2] Cf. 2 Kings xxiii. 11.

nection between the sea and the horse, but that
it has been thought necessary to attempt to
supply one. But let us take another animal—
the bull : there is a marked and peculiar connection between Poseidôn and the bull; yet I am
not aware that any particular link has been shown
to exist between the bull and the sea. The case,
however, presents no more difficulties than that
of the horse. Let fancy step in again, and
remind us that the roaring of the sea resem-
bles the bellowing of bulls, and the thing is
done. Now we may think we see why Nestôr
sacrificed bulls to Poseidôn on the sea shore.[1]
We might remember, too, that Hesiod[2] applies
the singular epithet Taureos to Poseidôn, which
some have with doubtful accuracy rendered bull-
voiced, and have then referred the term to the
roaring of Lake Onchestos in Boiôtia, where
Poseidôn had a temple.[3] With respect to this
alleged roaring of the lake, it does not appear to
have been noticed by several ancient writers who
have described Boiôtia, and, perhaps, it is merely
a conjecture to supply a plausible meaning for
the epithet Taureos. But what I wish to illus-

---

[1] Od. iii. 6.   [2] Aspis Hêrak. 104.   [3] Il. ii. 506.

trate is, that it is just as easy to establish a sort
of airy connection between the sea and the bull,
as it is to establish one between the sea and the
horse. The fundamental objection to such a
method of dealing with the question is twofold :
(1) That it is almost always mere guess work ;
and, (2) That this mode of treatment is far too
plastic, so that a connection or comparison of
some kind can almost always be drawn between
any two persons or things. Mr. Cox considers
Poseidôn's trident as a phallic emblem;[1]
but why, it is difficult to perceive. As possessing three distinct prongs united to one
shaft, Mr. Gladstone's conjecture that 'the
trident—an instrument so unsuited to water,
appears evidently to point to some tradition of a
Trinity, such as may still be found in various
forms of Eastern religion,'[2] seems far more
plausible. The trident was said to have been
given to Poseidôn by the Telchines,[3] an Oriental
race descended from him, and, like a branch of
the Kyklôpian family,[4] metallurgists and early
inhabitants of Rhodos (Rhodes), an ancient name

[1] Mythology of the Aryan Nations, ii. 115.
[2] Juv. Mun. 250.　　　[3] Kallim. Hym. eis. Dêlon, 32.
[4] Vide Sec. XIV.

for which was Telchinis. This is one of the
many links which connect the god with the
Hamitic East.

SECTION V.

NECESSITY OF DISTINGUISHING BETWEEN THE DIVINITIES OF DIFFERENT NATIONS.

Mr. Cox has ably illustrated the non-identity
of the Greek and Latin deities, and shown how
objectionable is the practice of using their names
interchangeably, which, among other evils, de-
prives the investigator of the valuable advan-
tages of comparison. It is ridiculous to call
Hellenic divinities by the names of Latin
divinities, when, in many cases, the two personages, thus blended into one, do not even hold
corresponding places in their respective Pan-
theons. Thus, for instance, Poseidôn and Neptune are frequently identified, when, in reality,
there is no connection between them. To take
another example : Mr. Ruskin calls Athênê 'the
Neith of the Egyptians.'[1] He may, perhaps,

---

[1] Queen of the Air, i. 14.

only mean by this, that Neith in the Egyptian Pantheon corresponded with Athênê in the Greek; but the idea conveyed to the mind of the reader is, that the two goddesses were identical, and that Athênê was worshipped in Egypt under the name of Neith. 'Egypt,' says Herodotos,[1] 'has communicated to Greece the names of almost all the gods.' He then mentions the few deities whom he considered as exceptions to this general rule, Athênê not being one. But his theory is unsubstantiated by fact, and Mr. Cox justly ridicules the absolute acceptance of 'the impudent assertions of Egyptian priests'[2] with respect to such matters. There is abundant proof of the Aryan character of Athênê :[3] she is not, therefore, in any way connected with the Hamitic Neith, and does not represent her, and this example may serve to illustrate the extreme desirability of distinguishing between the divinities of different nationalities. As we have now learned to call the Greek deities by their own names, instead of by the names of Latin deities, so there is no good reason for retaining a

---

[1] Herodotos, ii. 50.

[2] Mythology of the Aryan Nations, ii. 257.

[3] Vide Pro. Max Müller on Athênê, &c.

Latin form of spelling. The adoption of the Greek form may seem a little strange at first both to eye and ear, but we are rapidly becoming accustomed to it, and begin to wonder why the Latin dress has been worn so long.

SECTION VI.

NÈREUS AND NEPTUNUS.

THE Roman Neptunus, then, and the Greek Poseidôn, are two distinct deities; and the first remarkable point of difference between them, with the exception of their names, is, that while the former is a true sea-god, the latter, as Mr. Gladstone well observes, 'has in him nothing of an elemental deity.' The name Neptune is ' connected with many words that mean to bathe or swim ';[1] and so Col. Robertson says of the Nith, a Gaelic river name in Ayr and Dumfries: 'This river name comes from the designation of the god of the waters called *Neithe*, of which this one is a slight contraction. It is most probable the Cimbri, as well as the Gael, knew of the

---

[1] Cox, Manual of Mythology, 195.

C

water-god " Neithe," and also named a river after
him ; and Mr. Fergusson, in his work on " River
Names," refers to a representation found in
Tuscany of Neptune, and that the name written
over the figure was " Nethun," and gives as to
this name the following extract : " There can be
little doubt that *nethu* means water, in the
Tuscan language." The river *Nethan,* in Strath-
clyde, Lanark, is undoubtedly from the same
source, namely, from Neith-an, meaning Neithe's
river.'[1] So, again, in the Hellenic mythology,
Nêreus, eldest son of Pontos, the Deep, is 'the true
sea-god of Homer, who gave to the element of
water that name of nero, in the popular speech
of the Greeks, which it still retains.'[2] Thus
their names are illustrative of the characters of
Neptune and Nêreus, as the true Latin and Greek
sea-gods. And in the Hellenic mythology, besides Pontos and Nêreus, there is also the deep-
flowing Ôkeanos, sire of rivers, inland seas, and
fountains.[3] There was, therefore, no gap in the
Greek Pantheon which required to be filled by
another sea-god, and on all these veritable
marine deities Poseidôn violently obtruded him-

---

[1] Gaelic Topography of Scotland, 144.
[2] Gladstone, Juv. Mun. 243.   [3] Il. xxi. 195.

self, a circumstance which makes his position with respect to them somewhat anomalous.

SECTION VII.

POSEIDÔN THE BUILDER.

I SHALL now proceed to consider Poseidôn in his character of the god of building and fortification, a feature strongly marked and anything but maritime. He built the girding wall and erected the gates of bronze that shut in the penal dungeon of the Titânes.[1] He built the city and impregnable wall of Troy,[2] against which all efforts of the assailants were fruitless to the last. Nay, so completely was the art of building and fortification under his control, that, while the other gods, being indifferent on the matter, were admiring the newly-constructed wall which protected the Achaian camp, he complained to Zeus that the work had been completed without the offering of hecatombs to the gods ;[3] appearing to refer particularly to himself, as no other deity seems to have been interested in the question,

---

[1] Hes. Theog. 732. [2] Il. xxi. 446. [3] Il. vii. 450.

and implying that all builders were bound to show him special reverence. Zeus, in reply, appears to admit the force of his remark, and advises him to revenge himself by destroying the wall, which he afterwards did accordingly.[1] So his son, Nausithoös the Phaiakian, surrounded his city with a wall,[2] which is specially noticed as being a remarkable work. Pausanias[3] tells us, that all men know Poseidôn under the name of Asphaleios the Securer, an epithet given to him in allusion to the defence afforded by fortifications.[4] He is thus pre-eminently the building-god,[5] and it is in perfect harmony with this phase of his character that he is described by Homer[6] as being the father of Polyphêmos, the mightiest Kyklôps, and his savage brethren.[7] But in order to illustrate this connection, it will be necessary to review briefly the history of the three great branches of the Kyklôpian family, the Builders, the Pastors, and the Metallurgists.

[1] Il. xii. 27. [2] Od. vi. 9. [3] VII. 21.
[4] Cf. Strabo, i. 3. [5] Jur Mun. 245.
[6] Od. i. 73. [7] Cf. Od. ix 5 412.

SECTION VIII.

THE BUILDING KYKLÔPES.

THE principal examples in Greece of that style of early architecture which has been termed Kyklôpian, are the ruins of the cities of Tiryns and Mykênê. The former, one of the most ancient of Hellenic cities, and situated on a small hill in Argolis, not very far from the sea, was, according to Greek legend, fortified by the Kyklôpes in the time of Proitos, son of Abas, and thirteenth king of Argos. Homer alludes to it as 'Tiryns the walled,'[1] i.e., particularly well fortified.[2] Strabo[3] states that these Kyklôpes came from Lykia, and were called Cheirogastores (Hands-and-bellies), because they made their living by their trade. Pausanias, describing the place, says, 'The wall, which is all that is left of the ruins, is, according to report, the work of the Kyklôpes. It is raised from rude stones, each of which is so large that the least cannot be moved out of its place by two oxen yoked together.'[4] Describing the ruins of

[1] Il. ii. 559.   [2] Cf. Deu. i. 28; iii. 5.
[3] VIII. 6.   [4] II. 25.

Mykênê, he says, 'Among other parts of the inclosure which still remain, a gate is seen with lions standing on it; and they report that these are the works of the Kyklôpes, who also made for Proitos the wall at Tiryns.'[1] 'At Mykênê,' says the learned Fosbroke, 'was the "Cyclopean hall of Eurystheus"[2] and the sumptuous palace of Agamemnon; and though, as Thucydides[3] correctly says, the fortified town was of inconsiderable extent, yet it abounded with stupendous and richly carved monuments, whose semibarbarous but artificial splendour formed a striking contrast with the unornamented and simple style introduced after the Doric period.'[4] Homer describes Mykênê as 'the well-built city[5] adorned with gold,'[6] and Pliny[7] calls the Kyklôpes '.the inventors of tower-building,' a circumstance which will assist in suggesting a Greek meaning of the name. Fosbroke is of opinion that 'there were two synchronous styles used by the same Cyclopean workmen for distinct objects. One was of large cubic blocks, as at Mycenæ, for the royal cities of the Bible and the "poleais" of Homer; and the other, as at Tiryns, for "high

[1] II. 15.   [2] Pindar. Frag.   [3] I. 10.   [4] Encyclopædia of Antiquities, i. 7.   [5] Il. ii. 569.   [6] Od. iii. 305.   [7] VII. 56.

towers" and "refuges," the "teichea" of the Father of Poets.'[1] These Kyklôpian remains have frequently been considered to be of Pelasgic origin. 'The most ancient architectural remains of Greece are ascribed to the Pelasgians, and are cited as specimens of Pelasgian architecture, though there is *no positive authority for these statements*.'[2] I am not aware that there is any real authority at all for such statements, and on this point Mr. Gladstone remarks: 'The Pelasgians have been sometimes supposed to have brought the art of building with hewn stones into Greece. And yet the rival name commonly given to the ancient remains of this class is Cyclopian. But what is Cyclopian is, as we see from the Odyssey, immediately related to Poseidôn and to the cycle of Phœnician tradition. Now I think we may lay down this rule, that whenever Homer mentions solid building, or the use of hewn or polished stone, we find it always in some relation to the Phœnicians. Tiruns is "the well-walled." But Apollodorus, Strabo, and Pausanias report (in no conflict with Homer) that it belonged to Proitos, and was built for him by

---

[1] Encyclopedia of Antiquities, i. 4.
[2] Dr. Wm. Smith's Classical Dictionary: Pelasgi.

the Cyclops.'[1] It still remains a problem how
the huge stones used in all such buildings were
moved and fixed in their places; but, although
the civilised inhabitants of the East early
achieved marvels in masonry, what proof is there
that the comparatively barbarous tribes of the
West vied with them in the art? The Pelasgoi
were probably originally credited with the construction of Kyklôpian buildings because they
were supposed to have been the primitive inhabitants of Greece, and the highest antiquity was
attributed to such remains. It is not, however,
to the early Aryan inhabitants of Greece, but to
the Phoenicians, 'the missionaries of material
civilisation,'[2] and colonists, more or less, of the
entire seabord from Tyre even possibly as far as
Norway,[3] that we are to attribute these Kyklôpian
remains. And in so doing we shall be in harmony, alike with ancient authors and tradition,
and with modern research, and may well remember the positive assertion of Euripides, that
the Kyklôpian foundations were fitted together on
Phoenician principles, and by Phoenician tools.[4]

[1] Juv. Mun. 131.
[2] Lenormant, Ancient History of the East, ii. 205.
[3] Vide Sir J. Lubbock, Pre-historic Times, second edit. 69.
[4] Héraklês Mainomenos, 945.

SECTION IX.

PHOENICIAN ARCHITECTURE.

THOSE remnants of Phoenician buildings and works which have remained in existence to the present time, such as the foundations of the first temple at Jerusalem, and the great dykes and traces of fortifications at Arvad (Arados), exactly correspond in character with the Kyklôpian erections in Greece. Phoenician architecture, too, is remarkable, not only for its massiveness, but also for its compound character, as standing midway between the styles of Assyria and Egypt, and partaking of the specialities of both. 'Two civilisations of different kinds mingle in the works of Phoenician art, just as the manufactures of both countries [Egypt and Assyria] met at the same time in the markets of Tyre and Sidon.'[1] This rich compound architecture would doubtless impart that splendour to Mykênê noticed by Fosbroke, and well contrasted by him with the subsequent simpler styles that prevailed in Greece. For, the theory of the Oriental origin

[1] Ancient History of the East, ii. 232.

of Tiryns and Mykênê does not depend upon
ancient traditions and the testimony of historians; it is even far more apparent from the
character of the remains themselves. Speaking
of the building at Mykênê commonly called the
Treasure House of Atreus, Lübké says: 'A
brilliant coating of metal plates appears to have
formerly covered the lower parts. If we connect
with this the descriptions of the royal palaces, in
which Homer loves to indulge, where the walls,
thresholds, doors, and pillars glittered with brass
and precious metals, the relation to the customs
and art of Anterior Asia becomes still more evident.'[1]　And again, he notices that the base of
a pillar in front of the tomb is 'a purely Asiatic
form of art.' And again, when illustrating the
effect of Semitic and Hamitic influences on
Hellenic art, he observes: 'In certain forms
belonging to Greek antiquity we trace the
influence of Oriental art, transmitted to the
forefathers of the Hellenists by the trading
Phœnicians. This is the case in the capitals of
the columns and in certain ornamental details of
the Ionic style, which seem to come from
Babylonic-Assyrian models.'[2] 'Phœnician art,'

---

[1] History of Art, i. 101.　　　　[2] Ibid. 99.

says M. Lenormant, 'exercised a great influence over the first attempts of Greek sculptors. Among the works of the archaic epoch found in Greece, and all resulting from the teaching of Asiatic schools, there are some hardly distinguishable from Phœnician works, whilst others are almost completely Assyrian. All the first art productions among the Greeks have an entirely Asiatic character.'[1] The use of enormous stones, closely joined together without mortar, is a very prominent feature in Phœnician architecture, and, in working in stone, the Phœnicians were almost, if not quite, unrivalled. The very word Givleem, translated Stonesquarers,[2] is merely the name of the Giblites or Gebalites, the inhabitants of the city of Gebal,[3] and the Calkers or Chinkstoppers of the Tyrian fleet.[4]

SECTION X.

PHOENICIAN TOWER-PILLARS.

ANOTHER remarkable feature in Phoenician architecture is the use of round Tower-pillars, two

[1] Ancient History of the East, ii. 233. [2] 1 Kings, v. 18.
[3] Ps. lxxxiii. 7. [4] Ex. xxvii. 29.

of which appear to have been usually placed in
front of the principal entrance of a temple.
Such were Jachin and Boaz in the temple of
Solomon; and thus, Lucian, in his treatise, Peri-
tês. Syriês Theon (De Syria Dea), describes the
temple of Atargath[1] at Bambykê as having in
front two phallic columns, each thirty cubits
high, to the top of which the priests at times
ascended to converse with the gods. This custom
is further illustrated by Kyprian coins of the
shrine of Ashtoreth (Astartê), at Pappa (Paphos),
on which an isolated pillar is shown on either
side of the temple porch. All such erections,
whether actually towers containing chambers,
or merely 'stone cylinders, almost invariably
monoliths, terminated at the summit by a cone
or rounded cap,'[2] had, at once, a phallic symbolism and an astronomical use, while the
chambered towers also served as fortresses and
places of refuge. And, as it was customary to
erect churches and religious houses on the sites
of heathen temples, and in localities peculiarly
connected with the worship of heathen divinities;
so, St. Simon Stylites and the Christians of his

---

[1] Atargatis, 2 Mac. xii. 26.
[2] Ancient History of the East, ii. 230.

day endeavoured to disconnect the pillar from
its heathen, and to supply it with Christian
associations. It is not surprising to find towers
and pillars frequently taking a circular form; no
shape is more natural or more suitable for the
purpose. 'The eye is the first circle; the horizon
which it forms is the second; and throughout
nature this primary figure is repeated without
end.'[1] And not only pillars, but even cities,
were sometimes built in a circular form. Such,
for instance, must have been the shape of that
Tyrian settlement at Cacre in Italy, 'which
anciently bore the Phœnician name of Agylla the
Round Town.'[2] But perhaps the best example
is Ekbatana, which is thus described by Herodotos: 'Its walls were strong and ample, built
in circles one within another, rising each above
each by the height of their respective battle-
ments. This mode of building was favoured by
the situation of the place, which,' like Tiryns,
'was on a gently rising ground. The city being
thus formed of seven circles, within the last stood
the king's palace.'[3] But the Tower-pillar is not

[1] Emerson, Essays. No. x.: Circles.
[2] Rev. Isaac Taylor, Words and Places, second edit. 93.
[3] Herod. i. 98.

confined to the East; we meet with the form in
the West, in the celebrated Round Towers of
Ireland, and also in several places in Scotland,
such as Abernethy, in Perthshire.[1] Yet the style
and aspect of the Irish towers are altogether
different from the prevailing art and fashion of
the West. 'Almost all exhibit that peculiar
Cyclopian character of masonry, which has led
to such strange, though often plausible specula-
tions.'[2] Supposing it to be admitted that the
existing ancient round towers of Ireland and
Scotland were erected by Christians, and in
Christian times, the further question which remains for solution is—whence came the style and
shape ? It can scarcely be supposed to have
been originated by any early barbarous inhabitants of the islands; and, moreover, if the primitive Western Aryans had been accustomed to
build towers such as these, we might reasonably
have expected to meet with specimens of their
handiwork scattered over the whole extent of
their occupation. 'It must have been a sacred
and time-honoured form somewhere, and with
some people, previous to its current adoption in

[1] Vide Robertson, Gaelic Topography of Scotland, 75.
[2] Fergusson, Handbook of Architecture, 923.

Ireland.'[1] And who can have introduced it into
this remote region except the world-colonising
Phœnicians, the mighty masons, and veritable
Kyklôpes or Circle-builders? Not that all their
erections were circular, but that the use of this
form, as in these Tower-pillars, was an important
and peculiar feature in their architecture; and
one which, being altogether strange to the
Hellênes among whom they penetrated, the
latter, not unnaturally, called them Kyklôpes, a
name which may very fairly bear the meaning of
Circle-builders, since Ôps signifies, not only the
eye, but also the countenance and general ap-
pearance of a person or thing.

SECTION XI.

THE NAME KYKLÓPS SEMITIC.

If there had not been a strong primary connection between all the branches of the Kyklôpian race, so widely do the accounts of them
differ, that it might well have been considered
impossible to demonstrate any affinity between

[1] Handbook of Architecture, 920.

them; but fortunately we have a comparatively strong basis from which to proceed. The first connecting link is the name Kyklôpes itself, a very remarkable title, and one common alike to the Builders, the Homeric Pastors, and the Metallurgists. In the case of the Builders, we noticed that, coming as foreigners into Greece, they appear, in consequence of their peculiar art, to have been named by the inhabitants of the country Kyklôpes or Circle-builders. Kyklôpes, an Hellenic word, is, it must be remembered, what the Asiatic strangers were called, not what they called themselves; and when we find the same name applied to the Pastors, who, like the Builders, were foreigners and not of the Hellenic religion, and also to the Metallurgists, the assistants of Héphaistos, 'a god of Phœnician associations,' [1] we may be satisfied that it is the Hellenic form of some wide-spread Semitic name. This reflection also relieves us from mere speculation why the Kyklôpes are described by Homer and Hesiod as a one-eyed race. These writers have supplied an Hellenic derivation for the Hellenic form of the word; but, the word being Semitic, their derivation is necessarily as incor-

[1] Juv. Mun. 529.

rect in etymology as in fact.[1] 'One etymon,' says Fosbroke, 'makes Cyclopes a corruption of Cheklubes, or Cheklclubes, from the Phœnician *chek,* a bay, and Lilybeum in Sicily, where still exist the remains of the ancient walls, consisting of enormous masses of stone.'[2]   Though I cannot accept this 'etymon,' yet we are here, to some extent, on the right track; but I will postpone further consideration of the meaning of the name until I come to speak of the third branch of the Kyklôpian family, the Metallurgists.

SECTION XII.

THE PASTORAL KYKLÔPES.

HOMER represents his pastoral Kyklôpes 'as a race of shepherds, lawless, stern, and gigantic. Agriculture they neglect; they have no political institutions; but, living with their families in mountain caves, they exercise a savage sway over their dependants; they scruple not even to gorge

[1] As to suggestions in explanation of the single eye, vide Strabo, i. 2; Pococke, India in Greece, 37.
[2] Dictionary of Antiquities, 3.

D

their ferocious appetites with human flesh.'[1]
With reference, however, to cannibalism, it may
be observed, that although Polyphêmos devoured
several of the companions of Odysseus, yet we
have no reason to think that it was an habitual
custom of the country. Nothing is said about
the cannibalism of any other Kyklôps, and the
race habitually lived on pastoral produce.   The
Kyklôpes are, moreover, as before noticed, the
children of Poseidôn, and despise the great Aryan
deity, Zeus. Some allowance must, perhaps, be
made for exaggeration in the account which
Odysseus, who for 'strategic purposes' was an
almost habitual liar, gives of them, and also for
an air of monstrosity which is thrown over them
in consequence of the fiction of the single eye.
And with respect to the immense size of Polyphêmos, we may well remember the report of
the spies to Moses, that the Anakim made them
seem like grasshoppers.[2]   Next as to their
country. Thoukydidés[3] notices a tradition which
placed them in some part of Sikelia (Sicily), but
confesses that he knew nothing about the matter.
Mr. Gladstone, in his Homeric map, places their

---

[1] Pococke. India in Greece, 38.
[2] Num. xiii. 33.   [3] VI. 2.

country on the south-east coast of Italy; but, as I understand the Homeric account,·it was on the north coast of Africa. There is a general agreement that the Lotophagoi inhabited the Libyan shore between the Syrtis Major and the Syrtis Minor;[1] and Odysseus arrives at the land of the Kyklôpes after leaving the Lotophagoi, and on his way to the island of Aiolos. Kyklôpeia, therefore, may, I think, be looked for in or near the province of Africa, in the vicinity of Lake Triton, westward of which the Libyans were not shepherds;[2] but eastward as far as Egypt they led a pastoral life, living on flesh and milk, and, like the Egyptians, neither eating bull's flesh nor breeding swine.[3] This is in exact accordance with the habits of the Homeric Pastors; the wealth of Polyphêmos consisted in flocks of small cattle, sheep and goats only, and his splendid cream and milk are specially noticed. The inhabitants of the Libyan coast near Egypt did not eat the flesh of cows, on account of that animal being sacred to As (Isis); and so, perhaps, the Kyklôpes would not eat the flesh of oxen, on account of the connection of the bull with Poseidôn. The ox is an animal linked with many

[1] Herod. iv. 177.   [2] Ibid. 187.   [3] Ibid. 186.

Oriental religious associations.[1]   Again, the
Homeric Pastors are represented as inhabiting
caves in the mountain tops,[2] a natural position,
as being the best adapted both for observing and
repelling an enemy. But the situation of these
cave-dwellings suggests that they were, in part
at least, artificial; and the court before the cave
of Polyphêmos is described as being built with
hewn stones,[3] which were doubtless as in other
Kyklôpian examples fitted together without
mortar. In Strabo's time, caves similar to these,
near Nauplia in Argolis, were called Kyklôpeia;[4]
and the use of huge stones in their erections is a
most important link between the Builders and
the Pastors. Pausanias, too, speaks[5] of the early
Libyans as being ignorant of the art of building
cities, and as living in caverns. The position of
the Kyklôpes, the children of Poseidôn, in Libyê,
is also in exact agreement with the important
fact that Poseidôn was the great Libyan god.
Herodotos, in his careful survey of the Egyptian
Theogony, found in it personages who, in his
judgment, corresponded with various members of
the Hellenic Pantheon; but for Poseidôn, the

---

[1] Vide Juv. Mun. 322.   [2] Od. ix. 113.   [3] Ibid. 185.
[4] Strabo, viii. 6.   [5] X. 17.

Dioskouroi, Kastôr and Polydeukês (Pollux), Hêrê, Hestia, Themis, the Charites (Graces), and the Nêreids, he could find no Egyptian counterparts. He therefore concludes that these particular deities, with the exception of Poseidôn, are Pelasgian, that is Aryan; but, for their acquaintance with Poseidôn, the Egyptians are, he says, indebted to Libyê, where the god was first known, and where he has always been greatly honoured.[1] That Poseidôn was 'first known' in Libyê, we shall find reason to deny; but this testimony is highly important, both as showing the African connection of the god, and also as indicating the principal channel by which his cultus passed over into Greece.

SECTION XIII.

CONNECTION OF THE PASTORS WITH THE HYKSOS.

THUS we see that, as the Homeric Pastors were Libyans, so is their sire a Libyan divinity. But as the Pastoral Kyklôpes are, like their brethren the Builders, thoroughly Oriental in

[1] Herod. ii. 50.

their associations, the next question is, How is it that we meet with them so far west as Lake Triton? The answer to this is, I think, supplied by the history of Egypt. About the time of the Fourteenth Dynasty of that country it was suddenly invaded by the Hyksos or Shepherd Kings, a vast array of Arabians, Syrians, and Canaanites, especially Hittites, the Khitas of the monuments. After a protracted sway in Egypt, the Shepherds were finally driven from the country by Aahmes, the founder of the Eighteenth Dynasty. The majority of them returned to the East, whence they came;[1] but 'the discoveries of Movers have proved that at the time of the invasion of the Shepherds into Egypt, some pastoral and agricultural Canaanitish tribes continued their migratory movement towards the West, and advanced by land along the coast of Africa, beyond Syrtes and Lake Triton, and at last came to a stop in the fertile provinces that belonged afterwards to the territory of Carthage.'[2] On the north coast of Libyê, then, some centuries before the siege of Troy, had settled various wandering Canaanites, in which term may be

---

[1] Cf. Josephus, Against Apiôn, i. 14.
[2] Ancient History of the East, ii. 172.

included the inhabitants of Palestine generally. They were connections, or rather a portion, of the Hyksos of Egypt, a pastoral race, Perizzites or Dwellers-in-the-country. Many of them were doubtless of gigantic size, like the Rephaeem or Giants, the Anakim, or the Amorites, which latter tribe, although of inferior physique to the two. former, is, nevertheless, alluded to by the prophet Amos [1] as ' the Amorite, whose height was like the height of the cedars, and he was strong as the oaks.' Living quietly in a country of extraordinary fertility,[2] the Pastors ultimately degenerated into a species of patriarchal barbarians. Thus we see at the same time the non-identity, and yet the connection, between the Building Kyklôpes or commercial Phoenician colonists, and the Pastoral Kyklôpes or agricultural Canaanitish emigrants. I may mention that Mr. Cox considers that the Homeric Kyklôpes and their flocks represent dark storm-clouds and sea-mists. Polyphêmos, according to this view, is blinded when the sun disappears behind the sombre cloud. The sun, therefore, would seem to represent his one round eye; but this eye Odysseus himself blinded, and Odysseus,

---

[1] II. 9.   [2] Cf. Od. ix. 105–11; Herod. iv. 198.

according to the Natural Phenomena Theory, is
one of the numerous impersonations of the Sun,
who, therefore, in some unexplained manner,
blinds himself.[1]   It is extremely easy to ridicule
attempts to illustrate ancient history by means
of the Homeric Poems, but we must beware lest
our own explanations should be considered more
baseless and improbable than any historical conjectures.

SECTION XIV.

THE METALLURGISTIC KYKLÔPES.

WE now come to the consideration of the third
great branch of the Kyklôpian Family, the
Metallurgists.   The secrets of metallurgy were
among the numerous gifts of the East to the West.
M. Lenormant mentions the opinion which, he
says, he is almost tempted to adopt, 'that the
Canaanites of Sidon and Tyre first taught the
fundamental secrets of metallurgy in Western
Europe, and that the bronze age does not, as has
been supposed, represent the irruption of a new
race, supplanting the primitive savages of the

[1] Vide Mythology of the Aryan Nations, ii. 176.

stone age, but the era of Phœnician influence,
and the first developement of native art under
this foreign teaching.'[1] 'Their metallic productions are mentioned in the Egyptian inscriptions at the period of the eighteenth
dynasty.'[2] 'All the artistic articles of luxury
mentioned in Homer originate as a rule from
the men of Sidon,'[3] for ' his works of skilled art
are all of Phœnician origin or kin.'[4] Bearing
these facts in mind, let us consider the Metal-
lurgistic Kyklôpes, assistants of Hêphaistos, and
forgers of the thunderbolts of Zeus. Hêphaistos
himself is a singular compound of Aryan and
Hamitic elements; he appears before us in three
principal phases: (1) As simply representing fire,
e.g. Il. ii. 426; (2) As representing the power of
fire in art; and (3) As connected with the sacred
and symbolical aspect of fire. The first of these
aspects is Aryan; the other two are Semitic, or
rather Hamitic. It is beyond my present purpose
further to analyze the character of Hêphaistos;
but, among links which unite him with the East,
may be noticed his art as the great Chalkeus or
Metallurgist, his connection with the Egyptian

---

[1] Ancient History of the East, ii. 205.   [2] Ibid. 199.
[3] Lübké, History of Art, i. 63.   [4] Gladstone, Juv. Mun. 529.

Phtah and the Kabeiroi, his falls from heaven,[1] and his union with Aphroditê. He is truly 'a god of Phœnician associations,'[2] but there is no direct Homeric connection between him and the Phœnicians. The Hesiodic Kyklôpes are Brontês (Thunderer), Steropês (Lightener), and Argês (Bright One), Aryan impersonations of the thunder and its accompaniments, 'the dazzling and scorching flashes which plough up the storm-clad heavens.'[3] These are not primarily associated with Hêphaistos the Artificer, and only indirectly with Hêphaistos as fire merely; hence the silence of earlier writers on their connection with the god. But, when the conception of Hêphaistos as fire had become absorbed in that of Hêphaistos as the Artificer and Lord of Flame, then Steropês and his fiery brethren naturally become his immediate subjects and assistants. The Greek aspect of this changed Hêphaistos, Lord of Flame, is still comparatively simple, i.e. the power of fire in art; but, to the Hamitic mind, such a deity would also be associated with the sacred and symbolic aspect of fire.

In the Phoenician religion 'the element of fire

---

[1] Il. i. 593; xviii. 395. [2] Juv. Mun. 529.
[3] Mythology of the Aryan Nations, ii. 213.

was considered, in its most extended application, as the principle of life, the source of all activity, of all renewal and of all destruction. The solar or sidereal gods are essentially fire-gods. This clearly appears in Baal-Moloch and his worship, in which fire played so great a part. To the same order of conceptions belonged Baal Hamon, Burning Baal, the national god of Carthage ; another divine personage is Resheph, the thunder-bolt, the celestial fire.' [1] Akamas (the Unwearied) and Pyrakmôn (Fiery-anvil) are creatures ideal and imaginative ; but the Fire-god has suitable assistants, by the Greeks called Kyklôpes, which Semitic name I shall venture with Hislop [2] to derive from Khouk, ruler, [3] and Lubob or Lobh, a contraction of Lehovoh, Flame. The Kyklôpes, then, a term applied alike to the Builders of Europe and the Pastors of Libyê, were the Rulers-of-the-flame or Fire-worshippers. The Builders were Phœnicians and the Pastors Canaanites, both branches of one family, and alike addicted to an igneous cultus. The barbarous Libyan Pastors, however they might despise the bright Aryan Apollôn, would doubtless worship a grim Moloch,

---

[1] Ancient History of the East, ii. 221.
[2] Two Babylons, fourth edit. 374.   [3] Cf. Jud. v. 9, 14.

and, like the second generation of men of
Sanchouniathôn, stretch their hands towards the
sun, as the personified Fire-king. Such a cultus
would be at first incomprehensible to 'the Greek
mind, being the exact opposite of the associations
connected with the sacred fire of Hestia or Vesta,
the genial goddess of the hearth. And therefore,
on the advent of the Phoenician strangers, the
Aryan would not curiously enquire into or understand the meaning of the name Kyklôpes; but,
seeing their works, would explain it in his own
way, while later ages suggested the fiction of the
single eye. That the Hyksos were Fire-worshippers, and therefore that their priests were Masters-
of-the-flame (Kyklôpes), is certain, since Apepi
(Great Serpent), the Apophis of the Greeks and
last of the Pastor dynasty, is stated in the Papyrus
Sallier to have 'adopted Sutech as his god; he
did not serve any god which was in the whole
land.' Sutech or Set is identified in the inscriptions with Baal, and Apepi, like other Shepherd
Kings, is called 'the beloved of Sutech.' On this
subject Canon Cook remarks, 'If we accept the
probable tradition of Porphyry that Aahmes I.
suppressed human sacrifices offered under the
Shepherd Kings at Heliopolis, the form of worship

must have been Typhonian, and in all probability of Phoenician origin.'[1]   The system of Baalic Fire-worship conducted by its Flame-priests the Kyklôpes, was carried far and wide by Phoenician and Canaanite; and even in remote Scotland we meet with such names as Lann-gab-hadh-bheil (Langavill), or the Jeopardy of Bel (Baal), *i.e.* Trial by fire; Tulach-Beil-teine (Tullie-belton), or the Knoll of the Fire of Bel; Clach-na-tiompan, or the Stone of the Timbrels, *i.e.* those used to drown the cries of the victims, as was the drum (Toph) in Tophet, the Valley of the Son of Hinnom,[2] and many others of similar signification.[3]

SECTION XV.

CONNECTION BETWEEN POSEIDÔN AND THE PHOENICIANS.

IN considering the connection between Poseidôn the Builder and the various branches of the Kyklôpian Family, I have already, to some extent,

---

[1] Essay on the Bearings of Egyptian History upon the Pentateuch.   [2] Jer. xix. 4–6.

[3] Vide Robertson, Gaelic Topography of Scotland.

indirectly alluded to the affinity between the god
and the Phœnician nation. And although there
is no direct Homeric connection between them,
a circumstance apparently attributable to the
fact that it was probably from Libyê that his
cultus at first chiefly passed over into Greece, [1]
yet their indirect association could scarcely be
stronger than it is. This part of the subject has
been treated with such an exhaustive ability by
Mr. Gladstone, that it is almost impossible to
illustrate it further. The connecting links are,
of course, most prominent throughout the wanderings of Odysseus in the Outer World, where
Poseidôn is the ruling deity, and where the
Phœnicians, or nations and personages allied to
them, are almost everywhere exceedingly prominent. Here ' most of the Olympian deities retire,
for the time, from the stage. On the other hand,
the prerogatives of Poseidôn are enhanced; and
we even find him apparently presiding at an
Olympian meeting.' [2] ' In relation to the Outer
World, Poseidôn exercised prerogatives which seem
not to have belonged to him within the Greek
sphere. He raised the storm which wrecked the
raft of Odysseus; gathering the clouds, which

---

[1] Vide SS. xii., xix.   [2] Juv. Mun. 128; Vide Od. viii. 321, 344.

was the special function of Zeus, and causing the
winds to blow.'[1] Again, the link between Poseidôn
the Builder and the Phoenicians is so evident as
to call for no further illustration.   Mr. Gladstone
enumerates various historical instances of Phœnician connection with Poseidôn, as when 'in
the war with Gelon, Hamilcar, general of the
Carthaginians, offered to Poseidôn a magnificent
sacrifice, with a view to success in what were
mainly land operations.   Again while sacrificing
a boy to Kronos, he threw into the sea a crowd of
victims in honour of Poseidôn.'[2]   And he concludes that ' the Outer Geography affords us the
strongest evidence of the Phoenician origin of
Poseidôn.'[3]   With this conclusion, however, I
cannot quite agree ; the origin of the god does
not seem to have been purely Phoenician, nor does
his cultus appear to have been originally peculiar
to the Phoenicians alone, while at the same time
he was doubtless an important member of their
Pantheon.   And so we read in the Theogony of
Sanchouniathôn, which from its intrinsic character cannot have been merely an invention of

---

[1] Juv. Mun. 247 ; Vide Od. v. 291.
[2] Juv. Mun. 249 ; Vide Diod. Sic. xi. 21, xiii. 80.
[3] Juv. Mun. 248.

Philo Biblios :— 'From Pontos descended Sidon, who, by the excellence of her singing, first invented the hymns or odes of praise, and Po-seidón.' Here it would appear that, there being no Hellenic equivalent for the god's name, we have his Phoenician title Poseidón or Poseidaon, the meaning of which is yet to be considered. It is also stated in the same Theogony that Kronos (El, the Hamitic Ra) gave Bérytos to Poseidón and the Kabeiroi (Gibboureem, Mighty Ones). As these latter personages are undoubtedly Oriental divinities, the whole connection illustrates the Eastern cultus of the god. The savage rites by which he was supposed to have been propitiated by Hamilcar, speak of no innocent Zeus Ombrios, but rather of a bloody Baal-Moloch or Baal-Hamon, while the incident still further illustrates his Libyan sway.

SECTION XVI.

CONNECTION BETWEEN POSEIDÓN AND THE AITHIOPES.

AFTER thus noticing the connection between Poseidón and the Kyklôpes and Phoenicians, we

naturally proceed to consider his affinity with
another Hamitic race, the Aithiopes.   The
Homeric association between the god and this
people is as follows:—On one occasion, we are
told [1] that Zeus and all the Olympians, Poseidôn
therefore among them, went to visit the Aithiopes,
who are described as being blameless, *i.e.* without
fault in their duty to the gods.   There is here no
particular link between them and Poseidôn, but
the connection becomes at once apparent from
the Odyssey, where we read of another visit of
the god, alone, to this mysterious people, made
expressly for the purpose of obtaining their
worship, while the other gods, the Aryan divinities, remained at Olympos.[2]   His visit, on this
occasion, was to the Eastern Aithiopes; for it was
whilst returning westward that, from the mountains of Lykia, he beheld the raft of Odysseus
approaching the land of the Phaiakes.[3]   The
Aithiopes, we are told, are the last or most remote
of men, are divided into two parts, and dwell on
the margin of the Ocean-stream, some at the setting, and some at the rising of Hyperiôn,[4] the
Sun when on high, the exact equivalent to the
Hamitic Ra, who is strictly the Sun from sunrise

[1] Il. i. 424.   [2] Od. i. 23.   [3] Ibid. v. 282.   [4] Ibid. i. 22.

E

to sunset.   The Aithiopes, although divided into
two parts, yet all . alike live on the margin of
Ôkeanos, which, according to the Homeric system,
encircles the entire earth.   These singular statements, introduced with evident historical and
geographical intention, are, as we shall see, in
the main strictly correct ; a circumstance which
condemns the practice of treating Homeric
localities as either purely imaginary, or as not
belonging to earth.   In Mr. Gladstone's Homeric
map the Aithiopes occupy the entire margin of the
Ocean-stream from East to West, at the southern
extremity of the earth.   But this arrangement
does not seem to sufficiently divide them into
two parts.   The statements of Herodotos respecting this people are, in all main points, quite in
accordance with those of Homer.   The ' Aithiopes
of Asia ' formed, in his time, part of the seven-
teenth satrapy of the Persian Empire,[1] but they
are not longer considered ' the most distant of
men,' as the ' swarthy (sun-burnt) Indians ' lie
beyond them.   He alludes also to ' the Aithiopes
who border on Aigyptos,' or inhabitants of
the country commonly called Aithiopia, and to
the Makrobioi (Long-lived) Aithiopes, ' who

[1] Herod. iii. 94.

inhabit that part of Libyê which lies towards the Southern Ocean.'[1] This last circumstance does not in any way prevent the Makrobioi from answering to the Homeric Western Aithiopes, for the shape of Libyê, both in the Herodotean and Ptolemaic worlds, is widely different from the reality, and, in both systems, the Aithiopes occupy a vast region stretching in part along the shores of the Western Ocean. So Perseus, after having slain the Gorgôn Medousa, who dwelt by the Atlantic, in his flight naturally arrived at Aithiopia, where he married Andromedê. Virgil, as might be expected, faithfully follows the Greek writers. In his extreme East, next the Ocean, are the groves of India; in the extreme West, near the Ocean-edge and the setting sun, lies the farthest boundary of Ethiopia.[2]

SECTION XVII.

EARLY HISTORY OF THE AITHIOPES OR CUSHITES.

THE Hamites were the first of the descendants of Noah to found empires and to establish ma-

---

[1] Herod. iii. 17.   [2] Geor. ii. 120; Aen. iv. 481.

terial civilisation.[1] The First Chaldaean empire has now, contrary to the generally received opinion of the learned, been conclusively proved to have been Hamitic,[2] a fact never doubted by those who accepted the Mosaic account. But their pristine sway extended far eastward of Babylon, for the race of Ham 'exercised in early times an uncontested sovereignty on the coasts of Carmania and Gedrosia, along the Indian Ocean, and over all the south of the Arabian Peninsula.'[3] At the same time they spread westward into Libyê, and also established central Hamite sovereignties in Phoenicia and Canaan. Ultimately the Semites deprived them of the sovereignty of Chaldaea, Syria, and Arabia; while the Aryans replaced them in Persia and India. The name Ham signifies the Sun-burnt, and the term Aithiopes, applied by the Greeks to all dark races, has the same meaning. The Aithiopes are therefore the Hamites, or rather the Cushites, a family of the Hamites, the most remote of mankind in the Homeric system of geography, and are divided into two great branches, the Oriental

[1] Vide M'Causland, Builders of Babel, cap. ii.
[2] Vide Rev. Pro. Rawlinson, Five Monarchies, second edit. i. 43.
[3] Ancient History of the East, i. 58.

or Cushite branch extending eastwards from
Babylon and Arabia, and the Occidental or
Phutite branch extending along the coast of
Libyê. Homer does not include among his
Aithiopes the Mizraimic and Canaanite branches
of the Hamitic race, since he distinguishes the
Aithiopes from the Phoinîkes and Aigyptioi;
and it is this circumstance which makes him
represent the former as divided into two parts
separated by a large intervening space of country.
Part of the Cushite branch of the Hamitic family
settled in Aithiopia Proper, the inhabitants of
which are always called Cushites in the Egyptian
inscriptions; and these may be included among
the Occidental Aithiopes of Homer: so that
although, strictly speaking, a portion of the
Occidental Aithiopes were Phutites, yet the
names Cushite and Aithiop on the whole fairly
correspond with each other. The Oriental
Aithiopes seem to be alluded to in several
passages of Scripture, *e.g.* Ez. xxxviii. 5; and,
after these considerations, we can understand the
statement of Diodorus Siculus, that 'Tithônos
the brother of Priamos proceeded with an army
eastward through Asia, as far as Aithiopia, from
whence arose the story of Memnôn his son being

born of Eôs,' the Morning.[1]   The connection,
therefore, between Poseidôn and the sun-burnt
Ethiopians is another of the numerous links
which unite him with the Hamitic nations,
Kyklôpes, Phoenicians, Canaanites, Phutites, and
Cushites.

SECTION XVIII.

AITHIOPIAN THEORY OF MR. COX.

MR. COX would treat the Aithiopes (Ethiopians)
in a manner similar to his method of dealing
with many other nations and personages, i.e. he
would literally resolve them 'into thin air.'   He
observes: 'In the Ethiopians who fight at Troy
we find another people for whom it becomes impossible to find a local earthly habitation.'   On
the contrary, so many local earthly habitations
can be found for them, that we are almost at a
loss which to select.   'It may amuse historians,'
he continues, 'to regard this mysterious people
as the invaders and conquerors of the so-called
Chaldæan empire; but no historical inference

---

[1] For ancient comment on the Homeric Aithiopes, vide
Strabo, i. 2.

can be drawn .from any mention of them in the Iliad or Odyssey.' This should be proved, instead of being merely asserted; but, in truth, such proof would be impossible to furnish. 'We shall find the Ethiopians dwelling,' he tells us, 'not, as Mr. Rawlinson believes, on the south coast both of Asia and Africa, and as divided by the Arabian Gulf into Eastern and Western, Asiatic and African, but in the bright Aithêr, the ethereal home of Zeus himself, far above the murky air of our lower world.' [1] Independently of the historical objections to this view, it may well be asked,—If the Aithiopes are the inhabitants of ' the ethereal home of Zeus himself,' why should they be said to live at the two extremities of the earth, in the lands of sunrise and sunset? Why, if they dwell with Zeus, should he be said to go far from his usual abode to pay them a passing visit? Into what two divisions can any children of Aithêr be separated? How can they be said to sacrifice to the gods? And why are they particularly connected with Poseidôn? All these questions must be satisfactorily answered before the Natural Phenomena Theory, so far as it relates to the Aithiopes, can be accepted.

[1] Mythology of the Aryan Nations, i. 234.

SECTION XIX.

I HAVE noticed[1] the Libyc colony of the Kyklôpes, children of Poseidòn, and the statement of Herodotos as to the African antecedents of the god; and I must next briefly refer to the early connection between Libyê and Hellas, two lands whose shores are linked together by various singular ancient traditions. Thus Iasôn, when sailing in the ship Argô to consult the oracle at Delphoi, was said to have been driven by winds into the shallows near Lake Tritônis; upon which a Tritôn appeared to him, and, on being presented with a tripod, rescued the Argonaut from his danger, and prophesied that, when a descendant of any Argonaut should take the tripod from a temple near the lake in which it was placed, there would be an hundred Hellenic cities in that country.[2] Aristaios, who married Autonoê, a daughter of Kadmos the Oriental, the founder of Thebes, was a Libyan prince and son of the nymph Kyrênê, who gave her name to the

---

[1] Ante, Sec. xii.   [2] Pindar, Pyth. iv.; Herod. iv. 179.

district of Kyrênaia (Cyrenaica). With regard
to such traditions, M. Lenormant well observes:
'We cannot refuse to believe that they have
some historical foundation; this is also the
opinion of the learned Mannert. Their truthful
character is more firmly established now that we
are acquainted with the ancient connection of
Libya with Greece, and with the invasion of
Egypt by the Achæans, Laconians, and Tyrrhenians, by way of the western frontier of the
Delta, having disembarked in Cyrenaica.'[1] For
we learn from the Egyptian monuments that in
the fourteenth century B.C. an Aryan navy appeared in the Mediterranean, and a Japhetic
race invaded Libyê by sea, and settled near Lake
Tritônis, a circumstance which accounts for the
existence of this Aryan name in an Hamitic
country; as 'the fact that in the Veda Trita
rules over the water and the air, establishes the
identity of Trito or Tritos, the father of Athênê,
with Triton, Amphitritê, and the Tritopatores or
lords of the winds.'[2] The original populations
of Libyê were the descendants of Phut, dwelling
along the Mediterranean coast, the Gaitouloi

[1] Ancient History of the East, ii. 250.
[2] Mythology of the Aryan Nations, i. 440.

(Gaetulians), the ancestors of the Berbers, and who inhabited the more inland regions, and the Negroes of the far interior. Sallust[1] alludes to this early Aryan invasion of Libyâ, and styles the invaders Medes, Persians, and Armenians forming part of the army of Hercules.[2] The inhabitants of the country, he says, soon corrupted most of the foreign names: *e.g.* the Medi were called Mauri, Moors, and the various tribes were speedily to a great extent merged in each other. These Aryan invaders appear to have been of the Pelasgian race, and are the Lebu (Libyans) and Mashuash[3] of the Egyptian hieroglyphic inscriptions, in which they are also called Tamahu (Northerners), and Tahennu (Men-of-the-mist). The union of these Aryan tribes with the Aborigines of the country, wandering Canaanites (Hykso-Kyklôpes), and Phoenician colonists, formed the great Liby-Phoenician nation.[4]

[1] Bel. Jugurth. xviii.   [2] Vide Sec. xxxii.

[3] Maxyes, Herod. iv. 191.

[4] Vide Lenormant, Ancient History of the East, i. 259; ii. 236.

SECTION XX.

CONNECTION BETWEEN POSEIDÔN AND THE FAMILY OF THE VEDIC TRITA.

THE religion and Pantheon of such a compound nation would, of necessity, be also essentially compound; and the Aryan contribution to the list of deities chiefly consisted of the cultus of those beings, who, in Hellenic Mythology, are connected with the Vedic Trita, a ruler of air and water.[1] These are Athênê Tritogenaia,[2] the unvanquished and delighting in war; Amphitritê,[3] styled Agastonos,[4] the Moaning Sea,[5] daughter of Nêreus and Dôris, and sister of Thetis,[6] who, although not actually stated in the Odyssey to be the wife of Poseidôn, is nevertheless very closely connected with him;[7] and her son Tritôn.[8] Sometimes various Tritônes are mentioned. The Aborigines, Hykso-Kyklôpes, and Phoenician colonists, would supply the Hamitic element in Liby-Phoenician belief; and thus we see how the Aryan Amphitritê

---

[1] Vide Sec. xix. [2] Hes. Theog. 924. [3] Od. iii. 91.
[4] Ibid. xii. 97. [5] Juv. Mun. 345. [6] Hes. Theog. 240-3, 254.
[7] Cf. Od. iv. 385-453 with v. 421-3. [8] Hes. Theog. 931.

became the wife of the Hamitic Poseidôn,[1] who, by this alliance, is made the father of the Aryan Tritôn. 'For many centuries,' says M. Lenormant, 'the Pelasgi of the Archipelago, Greece, and Italy, the Philistines of Crete, the Sicilians, the Sardinians, the Lybians and Maxyans of Africa, in spite of this distance of sea separating them, united in a close confederation maintaining a constant intercourse,' and thus 'explaining the Lybian element, hitherto inexplicable, in the most ancient religious traditions of Greece, the worship of the Athenian Tritonis, and of the Lybian Poseidon.'[2] Having thus noticed the early connection between Libyê and Hellas, the introduction of the Posidonian cultus on the shores of the Aigaion (Aegaean) and Ionion Seas must next be referred to.

SECTION XXI.

TERRITORIAL CONTESTS OF POSEIDÔN.

ONE of the first features which attracts notice in the Hellenic legendary and mythic history of

[1] Hes. Theog. 930.   [2] Ancient History of the East, ii. 167.

Poseidôn, is the great number of territorial contests in which we find the god engaged. If he were a veritable marine divinity, this fact would be inexplicable. Why should a true sea god contend for sway on shore? Nêreus has no such contests, but is satisfied ever to dwell in his own watery depths; and the Hellenic deities generally do not struggle with each other for the sovereignty of particular localities. But we have already had ample reason to conclude that Poseidôn, although he has the strongest connection with the sea, is not an elemental deity or veritable sea-god at all. We observe him appearing as a stranger in the Hellenic world, intruding on the true Hellenic sea divinities, and at once endeavouring to gain a sway on land. His connection with the sea, so far as the Hellenic mind is concerned, is simply that he is a deity who has been brought into Greece from beyond it. Hence, although no true sea god, he is nevertheless always associated with the sea. Respecting his territorial disputes, a very familiar, but non-Homeric legend describes his unsuccessful contest with Athênê for the honour of naming Athens, the arbitrament of the gods in favour of the one who should produce the

most useful gift, and how the olive of Athênê
was preferred to the horse of Poseidôn. In
another contest with the same goddess for Troizên
in Argolis, a city named after a son of Pelops, he
was more fortunate, and succeeded in having it
named Posidônia; [1] and the two deities arranged
to hold it jointly, in allusion to which agreement
ancient coins of the place bear a trident *and* a
head of Athênê. Poseidôn had also a celebrated
temple, the same in which Dêmosthenês poisoned
himself, in the small island of Kalaureia on the
Argolic coast. This island the god was said to
have obtained from Lêtô, in exchange for his
rights in Dêlos. He also exchanged his rights in
Delphoi for the promontory of Tainaron in Lakô-
nikê, where he had another famous temple. [2] He
also contended with Hêlios for Korinthos, and
Briareôs, who was appointed arbitrator on the
occasion, assigned the Akrokorinthos to Hêlios,
and the Isthmos to Poseidôn. [3] He contended
unsuccessfully with Hêrê for her favourite Argos, [4]
successfully with Zeus for the island of Aigina,
and unsuccessfully with Dionysos for the island
of Naxos, which the latter deity named Dionysias
after himself. These are some instances of

[1] Strabo, viii. 6.　　[2] Ibid. 5, 6.　　[3] Paus. ii. 1.　　[4] Ibid. 22.

Poseidôn's numerous territorial disputes ; and the truth which underlies such legends is very evident, *i.e.* that, on the introduction of his foreign cultus into Hellas, it was everywhere opposed by that of rival divinities, most of whom were the already established Aryan deities of the country. These contests are unnoticed by Homer ; they were both unconnected with his theme, and were also all decided long before his time, in which Poseidôn was firmly established as an Hellenic deity, second to none save Zeus himself. The Great Stranger tells Hêrê that they two were much more powerful than the other Olympians, except Zeus ; [1] and although this line of the poem is by some considered to be spurious, yet, that Poseidôn made no idle boast is very evident, since Apollôn dare not even enter the lists against him in the Theomachy ; [2] Athênê shrinks from contending with him in the Homeric Outer World, in which he was all but supreme ; [3] and even Zeus himself is rejoiced when a contest between them is avoided, remarking, that he could not have compelled him to submit 'without sweat;' [4] whilst Poseidôn, on his part, boldly

---

[1] Il. xx. 136. [2] Ibid. xxi. 469.
[3] Od. xiii. 341. [4] Il. xv. 228.

asserts their absolute equality,[1] although when
calmer he admits the superiority of Zeus.[2]

SECTION XXII.

HIS CONNECTION WITH THE HORSE.

I WILL next notice Poseidôn's remarkable connection with the horse. We have seen[3] that
'his relation to the horse, which is very per-
ceptible, though not of primary rank in Homer,
cannot be adequately explained by any comparison
between that animal and the wave.'[4] The chief
Homeric instances of this relation are the statement that he gave the immortal steeds of
Achilleus to Peleus,[5] and the remark of Achilleus,
that Poseidôn must have taught Antilochos
horsemanship.[6] Also in the Homeric hymn to
Poseidôn, he is alluded to as the steed-subduer.
Mr. Gladstone has made a very ingenious suggestion in explanation of this somewhat obscure
circumstance, i.e. That the institution of Games
was Phoenician: that, being Phoenician, it was

---

[1] Il. xv. 166.   [2] Ibid. viii. 211.   [3] Ante, Sec. iv.
[4] Juv. Mun. 245. [5] Il. xxiii. 277.   [6] Ibid. 306.

presided over by Poseidôn: that the Hellenic
tribes, being much given to horsemanship, introduced the horse into the games: and that the
horse thus came under the special care and
patronage of Poseidôn.[1] With this view, however, I am compelled to disagree. For, I do not
think that the fact that Homer describes Games
among the Phaiakes in Scheriê is strong, still
less conclusive, evidence that they were an
institution originally Phoenician. We have also
a description of Hellenic Games in honour of
Patroklos; and, in the abstract, the Phaiakes are
almost as likely to have borrowed the custom
from the Hellenes, as the Hellenes from the
Phaiakes, and I cannot but think that Games
are an institution more Aryan than Hamitic.
Again, that the Hellenic tribes were much given
to horsemanship may well be doubted, both on
account of such legends as those relating to the
Kentauroi (Centaurs), which seem to indicate
that a man on horseback was regarded as an
unusual sight; and also, because it is evident
from the Homeric poems that the animal was
not much used for riding. Yet the fiery charger
that started up at a stroke of the trident of

[1] Vide Juv. Mun. 132.

F

Poseidôn was a war-horse, as truly as the splendid
steed described in the Book of Job; and it was for
that very reason that his maker was unsuccessful
in the contest for Athens, the olive of peace
being preferred to the animal associated with
battle. The war-car, so conspicuous in Homer,
was evidently first used amongst the Hamites
and Semites. The Egyptians, Assyrians, and
Canaanites were famous in early times for their
chariots and horses, and Herodotos [1] asserts that
the Hellenes borrowed the custom of harnessing
four horses to a chariot from Libyê. The four-
horse chariot was not unfamiliar to Homer.
Hektôr for instance had one, and his horses were
Xanthos, Podargos, Aithôn, and Lampos.[2] The
Phaiakian ship, too, that bore Odysseus to Ithakê,
is described as cutting the sea as swiftly as a
four-horse chariot.[3] Thus the war-car, like the
god Poseidôn, passed over from Libyê into
Greece, and hence the connection of the Libyan
Poseidôn with the war-horse. Yet, at the same
time, it must be remembered that Libyê was not
the original home either of the chariot or of the
god, but merely the channel through which the
use of the one, and the cultus of the other, were

---

[1] IV. 189.   [2] Il. viii. 185.   [3] Od. xiii. 81.

introduced into Greece.   This connection of the
horse with Libyê and with the war-car is in exact
accordance with the fact which Mr. Gladstone
has observed, that in Homer the animal is
nowhere mentioned in direct connection with the
Phaiakes, or indeed with the Phoenicians.   The
student of Homer may observe that, although
Poseidôn has a chariot and horses wherewith to
traverse the sea,[1] yet that, in the poet's mind,
he is too much of a sea-god to allow a description
of his using the chariot when on land.   Of
course the above explanation is open to the
objection that Herodotos only asserts that the
Hellenes borrowed the four-horse chariot from
Libyê, and is silent as to the two or three-horse
chariot.   But, as people who used four horses in
a chariot must almost necessarily have previously
used two, and as the whole combination of the
evidence generally, including the undoubted
connection between Poseidôn and the horse, is so
strongly in favour of a Libyan use of the war-car,
and of an Hellenic adoption of it from thence,
the strongest possible evidence to the contrary
must be produced before this view can be fairly
pronounced untenable.

[1] Il. xiii. 23.

F 2

SECTION XXIII.

HIS CONNECTION WITH THE LATIN GOD CONSUS.

POSEIDÔN, lord of the horse, seems also to be connected, if not identical, with the Latin deity Consus, who, by the later Romans, was identified with Neptunus, although originally quite distinct from the sea-god. Consus, an obscure divinity, was regarded as the god of council, secret deliberations, and mysteries; and also as the patron of horsemanship. In his festival the Consualia, horses and mules were freed from labour and crowned with flowers. Mr. Cox is inclined to connect the name with the Hindu Ganesa, 'the lord of life and of the reproductive powers of nature;'[1] but this is purely conjectural. Consus also curiously corresponds with Khons or Chons, who, in the Egyptian Pantheon, appears as the son of Amen-Ra, and the third person in the triad of Thebes, and whose name signifies Huntsman. Thus Khons, Consus, and Poseidôn are alike associated with the horse; whilst the attribute of mysterious wisdom which characterizes Consus, distinguishes Poseidôn in a similar

[1] Mythology of the Aryan Nations, i. 347, note.

manner; a fact not at once apparent in the
Hellenic Mythology, because this phase of
Poseidôn's character is much overshadowed by
the attributes of several of the Aryan divinities.
Thus wisdom generally is a special characteristic
of Zeus,[1] of Apollôn,[2] or of Hêlios the Sun,[3] who
sees and knows all things. But the wisdom of
these beings only represents the knowledge
derived from ocular observation, which is
perfectly distinct from the knowledge of mysterious religious secrets or other occult matters,
and therefore they do not, in reality, trench on
the character of Poseidôn in this particular, but
only appear to do so. In a remarkable passage
in the Iliad,[4] Poseidôn claims to be wiser than
Apollôn, who does not deny the assertion, and in
every way confesses his inferiority; while the
Subordinate (Hypodmôs) of Poseidôn, Prôteus
the Aigyptian,[5] is possessed of unerring knowledge and prophetic powers. We may fairly
assume that the master was as wise as the
servant; indeed he is expressly represented as
gifted with prophetic powers,[6] and it would seem

---

[1] Il. xiii. 355.　　[2] Hom. Hymn to Hermês, 535.
[3] Il. iii. 277; Od. viii. 302.
[4] XXI. 440.　　[5] Od. iv. 386.　　[6] Il. xx. 293.

not improbable that, although the Egyptians did not admit Poseidôn *eo nomine* among the number of their divinities,[1] yet that, under the name of Khons, he obtained a place in their Pantheon; as we shall find reason to believe that his worship prevailed amongst all the branches of the Hamitic Family, although he was known amongst them by different names. Consus, moreover, is regarded as a god of the lower world, or Chthonian divinity—another circumstance which connects him with Poseidôn, whose character becomes more and more Chthonian the farther his cultus is traced into the East, where also his phase as lord of knowledge and wisdom appears more manifestly. The name Consus well preserves both this idea and his connection with the horse; and it may be remarked, that the titles of the more mysterious divinities are generally found to be manifold in meaning. Consus in Italy, like Poseidôn in Greece, is finally regarded as a marine deity, because his worship has been brought into the country from beyond the sea.

[1] Herod. ii. 43.

SECTION XXIV.

HIS CONNECTION WITH THE BULL.

THE horse is not the only animal particularly connected with Poseidôn; there is also the bull, his favourite sacrifice; and the Homeric link between them is, in this case, quite as strong as in the former. Thus the Pylians, when about to engage in battle, solemnly offer a bull to Poseidôn;[1] and Têlemachos finds the Pylian Nestôr on the sea shore, engaged in offering a sacrifice of a great number of black bulls to the same deity,[2] who, as previously noticed,[3] is called by Hesiod Taureos, or Poseidôn-of-the-Bull. Thus, too, the Phaiakes offer twelve bulls to the god in time of alarm.[4] This connection is non-Hellenic, both because Poseidôn is not an Aryan divinity, and also because the sanctity of the bull or ox and its connection with deity is an essentially Oriental feature; reminding us of the Cattle of Hêlios, the Apis of Egypt, the Oxen of Solomon, the Calves of Jeroboam, and the winged Bulls of Assyria. Etymology may somewhat assist in explaining the ideas which seem

[1] Il. xi. 728. [2] Od. iii. 6. [3] Ante, Sec. iv. [4] Od. xiii. 181.

to have linked together Poseidôn and the bull. From the same Semitic root Sr or Shr come the words Sar, a prince or mighty one, and Shur, a word signifying both bull and wall.[1] Here we have a number of associate ideas : (1) A horn, the well-known Oriental symbol of power ; (2) A horned bull or mighty prince ; (3) A wall, connected in idea with a mighty man as being a source of protection. Shur, in Chaldee Tur, appears to have become associated in idea with the singularly similar Aryan word Taurus, Tauros, Sthûras, or Steer. And, as the Semitic root contains words meaning bull, tower or wall, and prince ; so also, curiously enough, does the Aryan, for among its kindred words are Tursis, Turris, Turannos, Tour, Tower, Tor (a projecting rock), with which latter we may compare the Hamitic Tzur (Tyre), a rock, whence the name Syria is probably derived. Tur or Taur-os, a word which might be understood to mean either the Bull or the Wall or Tower, and figuratively the Mighty One or Defender, is a term which could be aptly applied to the great and mysterious Poseidôn, the Building god, and known as Asphaleios the Securer ;[2] and hence, we see what a number of

---

[1] Cf. Gen. xlix. 22,   [2] Vide ante, Sec. vii.

ideas are combined in Taureos, the Hesiodic
epithet of the god. If, moreover, Gale,[1] following Bochart, is correct in the assertion that the
same Phoenician word signified both Bull and
Ship; the introduction of the cultus of Poseidôn
into Greece by means of ships may have been
commemorated by connecting him with the bull.
Occult symbolism has frequently availed itself,
either of two words of similar sound, or of one
word of manifold meaning, by commemorating a
personage or event signified by one of such words
or meanings under the form of the thing signified by the other. Thus, if the name of any
particular deity had the same sound as the word
meaning fir-tree, the representation of a fir-tree
was, to the initiated, the symbol of the god.

SECTION XXV.

POSEIDÔN ENNOSIGAIOS.

ONE of the ordinary epithets of Poseidôn is
Ennosigaios or Enosichthôn, the Earthshaker, a
characteristic the very opposite of a maritime

[1] Court of the Gentiles, ii. 1.

divinity. The most remarkable instance of the exercise of this power is in Il. xx., when the gods are preparing for the Theomachy:—

> Beneath stern Neptune shakes the solid ground ;
> The forests wave, the mountains nod around ;
> Thro' all their summits tremble Ida's woods,
> And from their sources boil her hundred floods.
> Troy's turrets totter on the rocking plain,
> And the toss'd navies beat the heaving main.—Pope.

Aidôneus himself, King of the Underworld, trembles; and leaping from his throne, shouts in alarm, dreading lest the Earthshaker should rend the crust of the world asunder, and display to gods and men his doleful regions. All this is indicative of a deity worshipped in a country subject to earthquakes; and so we find Strabo, after noticing how constantly the inhabitants of a part of Asia Minor, and notably of the city of Philadelpheia, were exposed to this phenomenon, remarks with respect to Apameia, 'For this reason it is probable that Poseidôn is worshipped there, although they are an inland people.'[1] As to Philadelpheia, the fact recalls the appropriate Apocalyptic promise to the Philadelpheian Overcomer, that he should remain an unshaken pillar, and should 'go no more out,'[2] i.e. into the open

---

[1] Strabo, xii. 8.   [2] Apoc. iii. 12.

country to avoid being crushed by falling buildings. The whole character of Poseidôn Ennosigaios is both quite unconnected with the sea, and
far more Oriental than Hellenic. We notice, too,
an inland worship of the god, which is to be
traced in various inland districts, as for instance
in Arkadia;[1] an additional illustration of his
essentially non-maritime nature.

SECTION XXVI.

OTHER EPITHETS OF POSEIDÔN. LORD OF AIGAI AND ΠΕΛΙΚΕ.

BUT considering the intimate connection established between Poseidôn and water, when once he
had taken his place among the divinities of
Olympos as one of them, it would be indeed
remarkable if many of his epithets were not
peculiarly appropriate to a marine deity. Thus
we find the god described as Gaiêochos,[2] the
Earth-encircler, in allusion to the all-surrounding
oceans and seas, although the epithet may also
have a further meaning.[3] He is also called

[1] Paus. viii. 10.   [2] Il. xv. 222.   [3] Vide SS. xxix. xxxix.

Kyanochaitês, the god-of-the-kyanos-locks; not azure-haired, 'for kyanos colour is that of dark-blue steel,[1] in allusion to the sea 'so deeply, darkly, beautifully blue,' and Amphitrítê is similarly styled Kyanôpês,[2] the dark-eyed. As having such an extended empire, both by sea and land, he is Eurysthenês,[3] the wide-ruling. As the builder of infernal prisons,[4] he is Pylaochos, Lord-of-the-gate, as Aïdôneus is Pylartes, Guardian-of-the-gate. I have already[5] noticed several places particularly associated with him and his worship; besides which, two of his most remarkable seats were at Aigai in Euboia,[6] and at Heliké in Achaia.[7] At Aigai were his palaces[8] in the depths of the sea, whence he drove his swiftly-flying steeds to a cave between Tenedos and Imbros.[9] His connection with gold, and hence with Oriental wealth, is remarkable. His splendid dwelling glittered with gold; his steeds had golden manes; he adorned himself with gold on setting forth, and his very lash is golden. With respect to Heliké, Homer alludes to the sacrifice of bulls[10] to the Helikônian king;[11]

[1] Vide Sir J. Lubbock, Pre-historic Times, 5.   [2] Od. xii. 60.
[3] Il. vii. 455.   [4] Hes. Theog. 732.   [5] Sec. xxi.
[6] Strabo, viii. 7.   [7] Il. viii. 200.   [8] Od. v. 381.
[9] Il. xiii. 21.   [10] Vide Sec. xxiv.   [11] Il. xx. 404.

and the place itself was overwhelmed by the sea B.C. 373, in consequence, it is said, of the inhabitants having refused to give up a statue of Poseidôn to some expelled Ionians. Near Helikê stood, at one time, a bronze statue of the god, holding a hippokampos (horse-caterpillar, 'the Syngathus Hippocampus of Linnæus') in his hand.[1] It is suggested that this little animal, the head of which when dried is said to resemble that of a horse, gave rise to the idea of marine monsters with the heads of horses, as attendant on sea divinities. Poseidôn was a favourite deity among both the Ionians and Aiolians; and his worship very extensively prevailed over Greece, the Islands, and a great part of Italy, as for instance at the celebrated city of Posidônia, afterwards called Paestum, in Lucania.

SECTION XXVII.

THE CHILDREN OF POSEIDÔN.

THE position of Poseidôn in the mythical Genea-logies of Greece is in exact accordance with the

[1] Strabo, viii. 7.

various circumstances which I have noticed as illustrative of his connection with the Hamitic East. Thus he is represented as being the father or ancestor of Bêlos, Agênôr of Phoinîkê, and Aigyptos; or in other words of the Babylonians, Canaanites (for the Greeks, very properly, made no distinction between the Canaanites and Phoenicians), and Egyptians, all Hamitic races. By some persons Hellenic Legendary Genealogies are regarded as utterly worthless and purely imaginary. It would be beyond my present purpose to deal with this question here : suffice it to say that, while such an opinion is necessarily incapable of proof, the contrary view is supported alike by reason, probability, and modern research. Through Aigyptos, Poseidôn became the ancestor of the noble house of the Abantiads of Argos; among whose members are the heroes Akrisios, Proitos, for whom the Kyklôpes built Tiryns,[1] Perseus, Amphiaraôs, the illustrious warrior-prophet, a descendant of the great seer Melampous, who is stated by Herodotos[2] to have brought Egyptian Mysteries into Greece; Adrastos, Alkmaiôn, and others. Through Agênôr, Poseidôn became the ancestor of Phoinix, mythic sire of

---

[1] Ante, Sec. viii.   [2] II. 49.

the Phoenicians, and of Kadmos, the stranger
from Kedem the East,[1] and the Labdakids of
Thêbes ; including Laios, Oidipous, Eteoklês,
Polyneikês, and Antigonê. In genealogical lists
and legends such as these, are preserved the
traditions of Hamitic immigration with its
consequent events ; and, while the stories of this
Elder Time are not to be received, in all their
details, as historic truths, in exactly the same
sense in which we believe the events of later ages,
yet to reject them as historically purely imaginary because, perhaps, many of them are replete
with difficulty, is highly unphilosophical, nay
ridiculous. Such a mass of legend and tradition
must have had some proportionate foundation ;
and it is the acknowledgment of this fact,
coupled with the difficulty of discovering the
foundation in actual history, that has led to the
Natural Phenomena Theory being stretched
beyond its proper limits.[2] Thus, in its utmost
extension, Perseus, Theseus, Kadmos, Oidipous,
Bellerophôn, and numberless other heroes, are all
resolved into the Sun ; and their opponents into

---

[1] Cf. Gen. xv. 19.

[2] As to its proper limits, vide Professor Max Müller, ' On the
Philosophy of Mythology,' Contemporary Review, December,
1871.

Clouds, Storm, Darkness, &c. This is the undue extension of the Theory. It may be applied with excellent effect to the Aryan divinities, and to various impersonations of nature, but must not be brought into history. The names of Vedic and Hellenic deities are, in many cases, undoubtedly mutually illustrative of each other; they sprang from one source, and point backward to a remote common origin. But, while we admit the original identity of Zeus and Dyaus, Ouranos and Varuna, we are not compelled to believe that Achilleus is the Vedic solar hero Aharyu, or that Odysseus represents the Sanskrit Ulukshaya, i.e. the Sun in his aspect of a wide-ruling power, Eurysthenês. True, the contrary is positively asserted; but that such an assertion is incorrect will, I think, be evident from a single example. To take the case of Zeus and Dyaus. Had we never heard of the Sanskrit language, we should, notwithstanding, be well aware, from Classical sources, of the place which Zeus, in the belief of the Greeks and Latins, occupied among Natural Phenomena; we should know that he represented

> The refulgent heaven above,
> Which all men call, unanimously, Jove.

This heaven must have been seen by all the members of the Aryan Family wherever scattered; and, as they all originally spoke the same language, and now speak kindred languages, it was natural, nay almost necessary, that they should call this universally conspicuous object by the same name, or at least by similar names. When, therefore, we find the name Dyaus in the Vedic Hymns, and notice that, not in name only, but also in mythologic position generally, he exactly corresponds with the Zeus of the West, we unhesitatingly identify the two. And now to apply this principle to the case of Achilleus, or any other hero. We do *not* know, from Classical sources, that Achilleus was a representation of the Sun; and, had the Sanskrit language been unknown, the idea that he is to be regarded as a solar hero would probably have never arisen. By what then is such an idea supported? By a very slight verbal resemblance, which, even if far stronger, might, as in a thousand other instances, be purely accidental; by fanciful parallels, often elegant and ingenious, but showing their inherent weakness as satisfactory evidence by their plasticity, and the ease with which they may be drawn; and lastly, by the

difficulties of an historical explanation. But all
these combined are far too weak for the purpose;
for, until we know from Western sources that the
Western Aryans regarded Achilleus as an im-
personation of the Sun, we are not justified in
assuming that the Eastern Aryans ever heard of
such a personage under any name whatever, or
that Aharyu is the Achilleus of the East. I trust
that this apparent digression will not be thought
unnecessary; for, if the Natural Phenomena
Theory be true in its extension—if Poseidôn is
Zeus Ombrios or any other Aryan divinity, then
the facts and circumstances which appear to
support his Hamitic origin must be illusory or
inexplicable, and the deductions proposed to be
drawn from them erroneous.

SECTION XXVIII.

THE CHILDREN OF POSEIDÔN—continued.

THÊBES being one of the most important of the
Phoenician colonies in Hellas, and Poseidôn
being a member of the Phoenician Pantheon, we
naturally find numerous traces of him in the

district of Boiôtia. Thus Asplêdôn, Anthêdôn, and Onchêstos, the mythical founders of the Boiôtian towns of these names, are said to have been his sons or descendants; and Aôn, ancestor of the ancient Boiôtian tribe of the Aones,[1] is also called his son. His temple and grove at Onchêstos were very celebrated.[2] Many other heroes and personages are called his children, as for instance Kerkyôn, a tyrant of Eleusis, killed by Theseus. This legend appears to commemorate some triumph of the national hero of Attikê over a foreigner. Poseidôn was also, as has been already noticed, the father of the Kyklôpes; and from him likewise were descended the royal house of Scheriê,[3] who ruled over that singular nation the Phaiakes, in so many respects the counterparts of the Phoenicians, and yet not absolutely Phoenicians. Various giants and monsters are also among his descendants, as Oriôn,[4] the giant-hunter of Boiôtia, a singular personage whose history seems to be borrowed from Oriental sources; and the Alôïdæ, Ôtos and Ephialtês, colossal youths, who at nine years old attempted to scale heaven by piling up mountains; which, says Homer, they would

[1] Paus. ix. 5.   [2] Vide Il. ii. 506.   [3] Od. vii. 54.   [4] Ibid. xi. 572.

have accomplished had not Apollôn slain them
while they were yet beardless.[1]   Mr. Gladstone
remarks that 'the efforts of the two youths
recall the traditions of the Tower of Babel;'[2]
and, in illustration of the connection between
Poseidôn and giants generally, it may be observed that, being a deity of the land of Canaan,
which was pre-eminently 'a land of giants,'[3] the
home alike of the Aimeem (Emims), Anokeem,
Rephoeem, Zamzummeem ('Buzzers'), Amorites,
and other gigantic races, he would naturally be
regarded by the Greeks as the father of those
races, in the same manner as they were the
children of Zeus.[4]   The myth of Orîôn seems to
have been taken from the history of Nimrod,
who is called by the LXX. the Giant-hunter.[5]

[1] Od. xi. 305.
[2] Juv. Mun. 251.
[3] Deu. ii. 20.
[4] Cf. Acts xvii. 28; Juv. Mun. 251.
[5] Cf. Professor Rawlinson, Five Monarchies, i. 154.

SECTION XXIX.

HOMERIC DISTINCTION BETWEEN POSEIDÓN AND THE ARYAN DIVINITIES.

BEFORE leaving Hellas to trace Poseidón into those Eastern regions in which he and his worship originated, it is important to remark the emphatic distinction made between him and the Aryan Divinities in the Homeric poems, which have all along served so well to illustrate his Hamitic origin. When Odysseus is in the Underworld, Teirêsias commands him to offer certain sacrifices, including a bull, to Poseidón ; and then to return home, and offer hecatombs to the gods who possess the wide heaven.[1]　Here is the clearest possible distinction made between Poseidón and the Aryan deities, who are constantly referred to as ' the gods who possess the wide heaven.'[2]　Odysseus is to sacrifice to all in order ; to Poseidón first, because he is in the Outer World, and therefore within the peculiar jurisdiction of that deity. When he returns home to Ithakê, i.e. comes within the regions

[1] Od. xi. 130.
[2] Ibid. vi. 243; xiii. 55; xvi. 183; xix. 40; xxii. 39, &c.

specially ruled by the Aryan deities, he is to sacrifice to them. When Homer wishes to include all the gods, he speaks, not of 'the gods who possess the wide heaven,' but of 'the gods who possess Olympos;'[1] that being a place where each god, and therefore Poseidôn also, had a particular dwelling or abode.[2] But it may be said that these distinctions are too finely drawn, nay, probably imaginary, and that the poet really intended, notwithstanding an apparent distinction, to include Poseidôn among the Heaven-possessing gods. Then I may refer to another passage, which, if possible, still more clearly illustrates the distinction.[3] Here, Zeus praises the piety of Odysseus, shown in his sacrifices to the Aryan gods, who are described in the customary formula as those 'who possess the wide heaven.' All the gods, except Poseidôn, pitied Odysseus;[4] and Zeus adds, 'But Earth-possessing (Gaiêochos) Poseidôn is ever angry on account of the Kyklôps.' Here Poseidôn the Earth-possessor, a terrestrial, not to say chthonian, deity, is contrasted with the Heaven-possessing gods. It matters not what signification is given to Gaiêochos; whether it be

[1] Od. xii. 337. [2] Il. i. 606. [3] Od. i. 68. [4] Ibid. 19.

understood to mean possessing the earth, in the
sense of encircling it, holding it in his arms as it
were, the usual meaning of the word when
applied to Poseidôn in his character of lord
of the sea,[1] a meaning, however, which would
appear somewhat insufficient in this passage ; or,
whether it is intended to imply that the earth
was in some special way his habitation, as the
wide heaven was the peculiar home of the Aryan
gods: be this as it may, the distinction between
him and them is clear and absolute.   They take
secret counsel against him, and it is stated that
he alone could not withstand them all ;[2] a
passage which conveys no slight tribute to his
power.[3]   He was not of the Aryan Family, and
scarcely acknowledged even Zeus as his Overlord.
He had ere this, by a conspiracy that was all but
successful, and assisted by two powerful Aryan
allies, Hêrê and Athênê, shaken for a time the
Thunderer's power ; and would even have succeeded in binding him, but for the interposition
of the hundred-handed Ouranid Briareôs, by
men called Aigaiôn ;[4] a singular story, apparently
illustrative of an alliance between the established
Aryan religion and an elder Nature Worship

[1] Vide Sec. xxvi.   [2] Od. i. 78.   [3] Cf. Sec. xxi.   [4] Il. i. 403.

against Hamitic innovations, which latter would seem to have been supported by an Aryan section of the community, as well as by Hamitic immigrants. Mr. Gladstone regards the legend as symbolical of an effort of anthropomorphic worship to effect the overthrow of a former Pelasgian creed.[1] Again, the hostility of Poseidôn to the Aryan gods is illustrated in the mighty effort of his children, the Alöïda, to storm the abode of the Heaven-possessors; a movement which, had it not been nipped in the bud, would have proved successful.[2]

SECTION XXX.

ORIGIN OF THE PHILISTINES.

HAVING now considered the worship of Poseidôn in the West, in Libyê and in Greece, it remains to trace it into those Eastern countries which were the original home of all religion and of all idolatry; for, although the cultus of the god passed into Greece chiefly by way of Libyê, yet was it not, any more than the war-car, indigenous

---

[1] Juv. Mun. 337.   [2] Vide Sec. xxviii.

in that country.   In illustration of the links
which connect the Eastern and Western shores
of the Mediterranean, I must now refer to the
composition of the Philistine nation, a subject
involved in considerable obscurity.   The very
early inhabitants of Philistia (Pelasheth), a
country extending from Japho (Joppa) to the
little River of Egypt, were the ancient tribe of
the Avim;[1] the district appears to have been
known at one time as Hazerim, or the Land of
Enclosures, and the Avim dominion extended as
far southwards as Azzah (Gaza).   The greater
part of the Avim were destroyed by the Kaphtoureem (Caphtorim), who came out of Kaphtour;[2] and mention is also made of the Isle
(Heb) of Kaphtour.[3]   This change of ownership
took place before the time of Moses, and the
first question which arises is—Who are the
Kaphtoureem, and whence came they?   That
they were subsequently known as Philistines is
evident from the question, 'Have not I brought
up the Philistines from Caphtor?'[4]   We find
the Kaphtoureem described as descendants of
Mizraim,[5] a name which seems to represent a

[1] Jos. xiii. 3.   [2] Deu. ii. 23.   [3] Jer. xlvii. 4.
[4] Amos ix. 7.   [5] Gen. x. 14.

race, rather than a man, *i.e.* Mes-ra-n, Children
of Ra, the Sun, which the Egyptians claimed to
be; and it is stated [1] that the Philistines came
or were descended, not from the Kaphtoureem
as might be expected, but from the Kasluheem,
another Mizraimic tribe. It has, however, been
suggested, and with much reason, that, in accordance with the passages quoted from Jeremiah and
Amos, the parenthesis should be transposed, so as
to read 'the Kaphtoureem out of whom came
Philistim.' The Philistines, then, would seem
to be a branch of the Kaphtoureem, or of some
closely kindred tribe; and, from the statement
in the Book of Genesis, it can hardly be doubted
that the Kaphtoureem were originally located in
Lower Egypt. But they are connected with an
island, and the name Philistines is rendered by
the LXX. Allophŷloi, Strangers. The greater
part, then, of the nation, but not all, came to
Philistia from some distant island, and we have
the choice of Kypros and Krêtê; the pre-
ponderance of evidence being, I think, greatly
in favour of the latter. The whole Philistine
nation, however, did not come to Philistia from
Krêtê; for there was a little Pastoral Philistine

[1] 1 Chron. i. 12.

kingdom at Gerar in the time of Abraham, composed doubtless of immigrants who had arrived
thither direct from the Egyptian Kaphtour.
The Krétan immigrants appear to have called
that island after their own name, Kaphtour ; and
Moses calls the Eastern Mediterranean the Sea
of the Philistines,[1] which may allude to a naval
intercourse between the island of Krêtê (Kaphtour), the Egyptian Kaphtour, and Philistia. The
identity of the Isle of Kaphtour and Krêtê
appears as follows : The Philistines came from
Kaphtour:[2] they, or some of them, are called
Cherethim or Cherethites,[3] i.e. Archers ; and the
name Cherethim is rendered by the LXX.
Krêtes : therefore, those who came from Kaphtour are the Krêtes, and Kaphtour is Krêtê, an
island ever famous for the use of the bow.   To
the same effect writes the learned Gale : ' The
name Cretes seems to be taken from the Hebrew
Crethi, i.e. darters, from their fame for darting.
Thence the Cretian bow and the Cretian arrow.'[4]
We observe, then, two distinct portions of the
Philistine nation ; the very early Mizraimic

[1] Ex. xxiii. 31.   [2] Amos ix. 7.
[3] 1 Sam. xxx. 14 ; Ez. xxv. 16 ; Zeph. ii. 5.
[4] Court of the Gentiles, i. 8.

immigrants from Egypt, and the mixed immigrants from Krêtê, an Aryo-Hamitic race.
Hence, there is no connection between the
Philistines and the Canaanites, and the conquest
of the latter by Joshua is regarded with comparative indifference by the former. With
respect to the Pastoral Hamitic Philistines,[1]
Herodotos[2] makes the singular statement, that
the Egyptians called their pyramids by the name
of the shepherd Philitis, who at that time fed
his cattle there ; thus illustrating the Mizraimic
origin of the ancient kingdom of Gerar.

SECTION XXXI.

THE EARLY INHABITANTS OF KRÊTÊ.

THE island of Krêtê was, at a very early period,
exceedingly populous[3] and powerful.[4] Homer
enumerates the following races as inhabiting it :
Achaioi, Eteo-Krêtes, Kydônes, Dôrieis, and
Pelasgoi.[5] Besides these the regular inhabitants,
there were also the Phoenician settlers on the

---

[1] Gen. xxvi.   [2] II. 128.   [3] ' Hundred-citied Krêtê,' II. ii. 649.
[4] Thoukyd. I. 4.   [5] Od. xix. 175.

coast, the founders of Phoinikê[1] and Itanos; and who are to be traced by such names as Lebena (Liar promontory), and Arados (Arvad), and by the discovery of ' a Cretan Jordan flowing from a Cretan Lebanon.'[2]　Three of the five races named by Homer, the Achaians, Dorians, and Pelasgians, were immigrants from Greece; there remain then the Eteo-Krêtes or Aboriginal Kretans, the Autochthons of the island, and the Kydônes, who lived near the river Iardanos[3] and were particularly famous for their skill in archery. The five races are all included under the general name of Krêtes,[4] but had different dialects; the result of which was that a mingled patois was spoken in the island.[5]　'The wealth of the hundred-citied island was just what might be expected to arise from the early combination of Phœnician enterprise with Pelasgian industry. There were many races in Crete, and there was a mixture of tongue.　This appears to indicate the presence of the Phœnician element in considerable force, with its Semitic forms of speech.'[6] Herodotos[7] states that the whole of Krêtê was

[1] Acts xxvii. 12.　[2] Rev. Isaac Taylor, Words and Places, 92.
[3] Od. iii. 292.　[4] Il. ii. 645.　[5] Od. xix. 175.
[6] Gladstone, Juv. Mun. 89.　[7] I. 173.

at one time possessed by barbarians, and therefore
we may fairly consider the Eteo-Krêtes, or original
inhabitants of the island, to have been the
Hamitic Kaphtoureem, immigrants from Egypt;
and this seems the more probable, since the
compound name Eteo-Krêtes, Original Cherethim,
is evidently a descriptive Hellenized appellation,
and not a title applied by these early colonists
to themselves. It may, then, be reasonably
concluded, that the Mizraimic Kaphtoureem
first colonized the island at a remote period,
and called it after themselves Kaphtor; that the
Kydônes, a Japhetic tribe of skilful archers,
subsequently established themselves in the north-
western portion of the island; that these two
races were both found there by the Phoenician
colonists, who, consequently, called the island
the Land of Archers, or Cherethim, which title
was Hellenized into Krêtê; and that, lastly,
other Hellenic tribes settled in the country.
The manners and customs of the mingled Krêtan
races would doubtless, like their languages, have
greatly assimilated during their joint residence
in the island; and the Kaphtoureem particularly,
being ultimately in a very decided minority,
would constantly become more Aryan and less

Hamitic, and so, at length, might entirely lose their Egyptian associations, and be united with the Hellenes. The country seems to afford an illustration of the combination of Aryan and Hamitic races, almost unique in its completeness, and it appears to have been the general base of Achaian warlike effort against Egypt.[1]

SECTION XXXII.

ARYAN INVASION OF EGYPT.

THE attacks of the combined forces of the Libyans and Mediterranean Aryans on the empire of the Pharaohs seem to have been chiefly comprised in two great efforts, a Western and an Eastern expedition; the former of which, although at first successful, ended in complete failure; while the latter, although unfortunate in its commencement, became finally a comparative success. The Western expedition, in which the combined forces of the Liby-Phoenicians, Achaians, Tyrrhenians, Lakônians, and Krêtan Philistines, invaded the western frontier

---

[1] Vide Juv. Mun. 145.

of Egypt in the reign of Rhamses II., the
Sesôstris of the Greeks, was at first successful;
and, at the close of his reign, the invaders
actually occupied the western portion of the
Delta; but, in or about the time of Merenphtah,
the son and successor of Rhamses, they were
defeated and destroyed. 'We need feel no
surprise,' observes Mr. Gladstone, 'at the silence
of Homer with respect to this daring enterprise.
He sang for the glory of Greece; and as on this
occasion, sharing the disastrous fate of their
Libyan allies, his countrymen were utterly
worsted by the foreigner, it was no fit subject
for his minstrelsy.'[1] Yet, as Mr. Gladstone has
remarked, there seems to be an indirect notice
of this invasion in the fiction related by Odysseus
to Eumaios.[2] In this imaginary account Odysseus
says that he sailed with nine ships from Krêtê
to Aigyptos, a voyage occupying five days; that,
when arrived in Aigyptos, his comrades began to
plunder the country and murder the inhabitants;
that an Aigyptian force was collected, and a
battle ensued in which the Krêtans were completely routed; and that he himself was taken
prisoner with others, and made to work for the

[1] Juv. Mun. 146. [2] Od. xiv.

Aigyptians.[1] His fiction thus exactly agrees
with the historical account of this unsuccessful
Libyo-Aryan invasion of Egypt; which it would
appear, therefore, Homer must have had in view
when putting the story into the mouth of
Odysseus. The notice of the severe bondage to
which the captives were condemned, both reminds us of the sufferings of the Israelites, and
is peculiarly connected with the era of Sesôstris;
during which Egypt was crushed under the
oppression of a building mania, the intensity of
which is almost unparalleled in history.

SECTION XXXIII.

SETTLEMENT OF THE KRÊTES IN PHILISTIA.

THE Eastern expedition against Egypt from
Krêtê resulted in the settlement of the Krêtan
Philistines in the south-west portion of the land
of Canaan. At the time of the death of Joshua,
the Primitive Philistines or Mizraimic Pastors
were unsubdued;[2] and were then established in
the five cities of Gaza, Ashdod, Askelon, Gath, and

[1] Od. xiv. 272.   [2] Jos. xiii. 2, 3; xxiii. 4.

H

Ekron. Soon after, the Tribe of Judah took Gaza, Askelon, and Ekron,[1] but it does not appear that Ashdod and Gath were ever subdued by the Israelites. Thus the remnant of Philistines remained [2] surrounded on all sides by the victorious invaders, who must inevitably have crushed them, had it not been for unexpected assistance from Krêtê. The next notice of them is in the account of the exploit of Shamgar, who slew six hundred Philistines with an ox goad.[3] After a very considerable interval, the almost annihilated nation appear again upon the scene; but this time under a very different aspect, namely, as oppressing Israel after the death of Jair,[4] and some years later we find Israel under a Philistine servitude which lasted for forty years.[5] The monuments of Egypt have revealed to us the cause of these remarkable changes in the balance of power. Undaunted by their Egyptian defeats, the Aryans of south-eastern Europe prepared to renew the war in another quarter; and allying themselves with the Khitas (Hittites), an exceedingly powerful people inhabiting the country immediately north of

[1] Jud. i. 18.   [2] Ibid. iii. 3.   [3] Ibid. 31.
[4] Ibid. x. 7, 8.   [5] Ibid. xiii. 1.

Palestine, they made a descent on a large scale on the south-west coast, where the Hamitic Philistines were already established. The reigning Egyptian sovereign was Rhamses III., a great military monarch, whose army, marching with the utmost rapidity, succeeded in defeating the Allies in detail. The Pharaoh first routed the Khitas, and then, hastening southwards, he surrounded and overpowered the newly arrived Krêtan immigrants, who appear, from the sculptures, to have been accompanied by their wives and children. 'In consequence of this victory over the Philistines,' says M. Lenormant, 'Ramses found an entire nation prisoners in his hands, and was compelled to assign them lands in his dominions, thus realizing the object of their emigration.' He therefore settled them near Gaza, Ashdod, and Askelon. 'There it was that, strengthened by new immigrations from Crete, they, in the decline of the Egyptian monarchy, founded a state so formidable for some time to the Israelites and Phœnicians.'[1] . Thus the early Sidonian supremacy was terminated by the destruction of that city by the Philistines about B.C. 1200. Lastly, with respect

[1] Ancient History of the East, i. 267.

to the name Philistine. As the nation was composed of two elements, the Primitive Hamitic Pastors and the Aryan invaders, so the name may, naturally, be expected to have more meanings than one. With respect to the Pastors, I have noticed the legend of Herodotos about the Egyptian Shepherd Philitis; and the name Philitis is said to signify Shepherd, in which case Palestina, the Land of the Philistines,[1] is Pali-stan, the Land of Shepherds, the Palaistinoi of Josephus. As to the Aryan branch of the nation, the name Pilistin or Philistin is said to be akin to Pelasgoi, as containing the same essential elements,[2] and to signify Strangers. The Kaphtoureem and Kydônes already settled in Krêtê may, naturally, have so called the subsequent Pelasgian colonists; and the Palaistinoi or Shepherds, with the Allophŷloi or Strangers, together composed the Philistine nation.[3]

[1] Cf. Zeph. ii. 6.
[2] Ancient History of the East, i. 123.
[3] Vide Rev. I. Taylor, Words and Places, 61, 72.

SECTION XXXIV.

POSEIDÔN AS DAGON.

The previous investigations respecting the Philistines are for the purpose of illustrating the close
connection which existed between the shores of the
Mediterranean; that is, between the various tribes
of the Greeks, the Tyrrhenians, Phoenicians, Liby-
Phoenicians, and Egyptians. All these nations
were well acquainted with the great deity
Poseidôn, and all, except the Egyptians, were
his worshippers; even they probably worshipped
him under another form.[1] Gale supposes that
the name Poseidôn is equivalent to the Punic
Pesitan, which signifies 'expanse' or 'breadth,'
and which he applies to the god as *laté imperans*,
the Wide-ruling; a circumstance alluded to in
the epithet Eurysternos,[2] Broad-breasted, and not
necessarily confined to sway on sea. This supposition, although probably incorrect, is, nevertheless, far more plausible than the watery
conjectures of Platôn and others. The Posei-
dônian cultus would be introduced into Krêtê,

[1] Cf. Sec. xxiii.   [2] Il. ii. 478.

alike from Libyê and from Phoenicia; and thus
Africa and Asia would bring into Europe the
worship of a deity, originally Asiatic, derivatively
African, and ultimately Hellenic.   We have
traced the Krêtan Philistines into Palestine;
and as, doubtless, they were not in such a hurry
when embarking as to leave their deities and
religious belief behind them, we naturally expect
to find the cultus of Poseidôn on the south-
eastern shores of the Mediterranean, and there it
is to be found accordingly; the god occupied the
first place in the Pantheon of the 'mingled
people' of Krêtê, and he retains his supremacy
in Philistia under the familiar title of Dagon,
which, as will be seen, is only a variation of the
Phoeniko-Hellenic name. · It is evident that
Dagon was the chief and head of Philistine
deities.   It was in his temple that the Philistines gathered on the great occasion of the
capture of Samson, to sacrifice and to rejoice;
and it was to Dagon, the national god, that the
glory of the overthrow of the mighty Hebrew
was ascribed.[1]   It was in his temple also that
Saul's head was placed;[2] and, in triumphing over
Dagon on the occasion of the capture of the ark,

---

[1] Jud. xvi. 23.   [2] 1 Chron. x. 10.

the superiority of the God of Israel over the
inferior members of the Philistine Theogony was
shown to be complete. Of course Poseidôn, *eo
nomine*, is never represented in Dagonic form,
i.e. as a man-fish; or, as a man with the upper
part of his body issuing out of a fish's mouth;
or, as a man with a fish's head over his head and
its tail hanging down his back; because Greek
art and Greek mythology are essentially anthropomorphic with respect to their divinities. The
Greek mind accepts the idea of monsters, numerous and horrible, but never forgets that they
are monsters: to the Hamitic mind, monsters
are often gods. As, according to the Chaldæan
account of the pristine chaos, monsters with
men's heads and animals' bodies, or the opposite,
or with different parts of various animals combined in one form, swarmed in the darkness and
water; so did the Hamites and Assyrians often
represent their deities as ram-headed, hawk-
headed, or cow-headed human forms; or, conversely, as man-headed beasts, or under other
forms not human. The history and ideas commemorated under the form of Dagon are of an
earlier date than the palmy days of Philistine
power; they even take us back to the period of

the Deluge; and an analysis of Dagon-worship will show that, although like Poseidón he is a deity connected with the sea, yet that, also like him, he is not a veritable sea-god.

SECTION XXXV.

DAGON AND SIDON.

BUT since the facts that Poseidón was the head of the Libyo-Krêtan Pantheon; that the greater part of the Philistine nation were Krêtan emigrants; that Dagon was the head of the Philistine Pantheon; and lastly, that, in essentials, there is a strong resemblance between the two deities when we divest Poseidón of his Aryan trappings, and those features of his character which are produced by his antagonism with the Aryan divinities are not absolutely conclusive, though exceedingly strong prima facie evidence, of the identity of the lords of Aigai and Ashdod; yet certainty will, I think, be obtained by coupling these circumstances with the result of the analysis of their names. The name Da -on or Dagaun signifies the fish Aun. Did the Philistines,

an Aryo-Hamitic race, call their deity by this
name, which would imply their use of the Semitic
word Dag, Fish? Doubtless it is perfectly possible that they did, but I am inclined to think not,
for several reasons; and that this name, as far as
the first syllable is concerned, is a Semitic translation of an Hamitic word, in the same manner
as Jeremiah[1] translates the Hamitic On by the
corresponding Semitic name Bethshemesh. The
worship of Dagon was not confined to Philistia:
thus Professor Rawlinson[2] alludes to him as 'the
Phoenician Dagon.' This brings us to the consideration of the Phoenician name Sidon or Sid-
aun, of which there are several interpretations,
all, however, illustrative of the connection of the
name with Dagon. Thus, it is said that the
name Sidon signifies Fishing-station, like Beth-
saida, the House of Fish;[3] while Charles Taylor,
the Editor of Calmet's 'Dictionary of the Bible,'
of whose learned labours on this point I have
availed myself, analyzes the word into Tzidé-aun.
Tzi is a decked ship, and Dé the Chaldaic Da,
The. Saida, therefore, is The Ship, and Si-da-aun
is the Ship Aun or Ship of Aun. Philo Byblius

[1] XLIII. 13.   [2] Ancient Monarchies, ii. 14.
[3] Rev. Is. Taylor, Words and Places, 90.

expressly states that 'Dag-aun is Sidon'; by which he implies that the Dag, the Fish, was equivalent in symbolism with the Tzi, the Ship, and that the words might be used interchangeably. This materially strengthens the supposition that Dagon is the Semitic name for the Hamitic Seidon, the connection between which name and the Phoenician Po-sei-dôn is sufficiently evident. In the Phoenician Cosmogony, to Dagon, *i.e.* to the Aun of the Fish, is attributed the discovery of wheat and of the plough— a circumstance easily explained by the history of this mysterious Aun, which must next be noticed. It will be remarked that Poseidôn, as Dagon, is disunited from his Aryan consort, Amphitritê, and becomes connected with a more suitable mate, Derketô, the Mermaid of Askelon, also called Atergatis (Atergath), who is stated by Lucian[1] to have been represented as a woman-fish.

[1] Peri. tês. Syr. The.

SECTION XXXVI.

THE AUN.

By the An, Aun, or Aön, called the Aun of the Fish and of the Ship, Dag-Aun and Sid-Aun, we must necessarily understand the human being thus represented as dwelling in the Fish and Ship; as one Dagonic form represents a man with the upper part of his body issuing out of a fish's mouth, and another a man clad with a fish as with a cloak.[1] This human being I shall notice more particularly when speaking of the Chaldaean Oannês; but the question which next arises is: What is the meaning of the word Aun? On or An frequently appears as a termination of ancient names of places or persons in a Semitic or Hamitic connection: thus, Babyl-on, which is the Semitic Bab-Il or Gate of God, a form equivalent to the Hamitic Ka-Ra, with the termination Aun. So Hebr-on, otherwise Kirjath-Arba, El-on, Herm-on, Sid-on, Poseid-on, Dag-on, Beth-Aven, i.e. Aun, 'the sin of Israel';[2] and in Phoenician Boiôtia, too, the termination is frequent, as A-on, ancestor of the Aon-es,

---

[1] SS. xxxiv. xxxvii.   [2] Hos. x. 8.

Aspled-on, Anthed-on, Ori-on, all children of
Poseid-on; nor is it wanting in Philistia, where
examples are found in Ekr-on and Askel-on;
while lastly, Egypt supplies Zo-an (Tanis), Zeph-
on, and the name of On or Aun itself. The meaning of the name of the Egyptian city of On must,
therefore, be ascertained. Moses tells us that Jo-
seph married Asenath (As-Neith or Isis-Neith), the
daughter of Poti-pherah (Pati-para, *i.e.* Devoted
to Ra, the Sun), priest of On or Aun; [1] which the
LXX. render Heliopolis, City of the Sun, while
Jeremiah [2] calls the city, the Egyptian name of
which seems to have been Ei-Ra, by the equivalent Semitic title of Beth-shemesh, or House of
Shamas, [3] the Sun. Beth-shemesh, 'the true
sacerdotal city and university of Northern
Egypt,' [4] was famous for its solar worship; [5] but
it will be observed that Aun is not the name of
the place, but of the deity to whom Poti-pherah
was devoted. That deity was Ra, the Sun; yet
Aun-worship was not merely a simple solar cultus.
The word itself has both a Semitic and an
Hamitic meaning. Its Mizraimic signification
is the Enlightener; probably in the sense of a

[1] Gen. xli. 45.   [2] xliii. 13.   [3] Cf. Chemosh.
[4] Ewald.   [5] Herod. ii. 59, 73.

teacher or instructor, of whom the Sun is the
natural type. Hence, Aun-worship easily degenerated into mere Sun-worship; as the symbol is
constantly confounded with the thing signified.
The Semitic root An signifies primarily ' labour '
or ' energy,' especially procreative power; in
which sense the word is used in such passages
as Gen. xlix. 3, and Deu. xxi. 17. Hence, the
Aun is the great Enlightener or Teacher, and
also the Procreator of all, from whom all spring
or are descended : according to the saying Omnia
ex ovo, All things from the egg, Òön, Aun. But
why should the seat of Aun-worship be placed at
Ei-Ra, the Abode of the Sun? For a twofold
reason. First, because the Sun is the great
vivifying and procreative power in nature,[1] and
therefore fit symbol of the Aun; and, secondly,
because the Aun, the Enlightener, as the great
sire of all, was necessarily the instructor and
moral and intellectual Illuminator of men, as
the Sun was their physical illuminator. Here,
again, the symbolism holds good; but be it remembered that the Aun is not the Sun, nor is
Aun-worship merely solar idolatry, although
probably, especially in its later stages, that was

[1] Cf. Mythology of the Aryan Nations, ii. 102.

its character in the eyes of the ignorant many.
With the word Aun may be compared the mystic
Hindu word Om or Aum, expressive of divinity
and creative power; which probably appears in
some Greek words in the form of On and Om: the
letters M and N, it may be observed, are often
interchanged in the Hebrew, as having a somewhat similar sound. All the descendants of Noah
would have equal reason to commemorate the
Aun.

SECTION XXXVII.

THE LEGEND OF OANNÊS.

IN further illustration of the subject, I may now
refer to the familiar legend of the Chaldaean
Oannês, which is briefly as follows:—In the
earliest times there came up from the waters of
the Red Sea (*i.e.*, the Erythraeum Mare, now
forming part of the Indian Ocean) a Creature
truly wise, called Oannês, having the whole body
of a fish, and above the head rose another head;
it had feet like a man, which came out from the
tail of the fish. It had a human voice and language, and remained on shore during the day,

teaching the natives letters and the arts of civilisation generally, how to build cities, raise temples
to the Deity, make laws, study geometry, and
conduct agricultural operations. At sunset the
Creature plunged into the sea, and passed the
night there. Afterwards several similar creatures appeared, one of whom was called Ho
Dagôn, The Dagon. Helladius, a writer of the
fourth century, a few fragments of whose works
have been preserved in quotations, after noticing
the legend, states that this Creature, whom he
calls Oän, had human feet and hands, and indeed
was altogether a man ; but that he appeared like
a fish because he was covered with the skin of a
fish. Some said he was born of the first parent,
which is the Egg. This last statement reminds
us of the legend of Hyginus, a writer of uncer-
tain date, the author of a collection of mytho-
logical stories, about the vast egg which was
said to have fallen from heaven into the Eu-
phrates, and to have been conducted to the shore
by fishes, who, for their efforts on the occasion,
were translated to the skies, where they became
the constellation and zodiacal sign Pisces. The
chief authors who notice the Legend of Oannés
are Bêrôsos, the Babylonian priest of Bel, who

lived about B.C. 250, and fragments of whose
Greek History of Babylonia are preserved in
Josephus, Eusebius, Syncellus, and others, Apollo-
dôros, and Helladius, fragments of whose works
are preserved in the Myriobiblon of Phôtios,
Patriarch of Constantinople, who lived in the
ninth century.[1] Next, as to the meaning of the
word Oannês, Taylor [2] explains the Oän of Helladius as Ho Aun, The Aun; and Oannês as the
Aun of the Nês (Nêos), i.e., Naus, Navis, or Ship,
that is, the Aun of the Ship. Such an interpretation is in exact accordance with the names
Dag-Aun and Sid-Aun, the Aun of the Fish and of
the Ship; but is open to the serious objection that
the name, which Bêrôsos puts into a Greek form
as Oannês, being some Semitic or Hamitic word,
cannot have an Aryan derivation. It will, however, probably be at once admitted that the Oän
of Helladius is identical with the Oän-nês of
Bêrôsos, and that both represent the Aun of
Ei-ra (Hêliopolis). Some other interpretation,
therefore, must be found for the final syllable of
the word Oannês. Hislop, in an ingenious work,[3]

---

[1] As to Mediæval Dagonism, vide Rabelais, iv. 38 ; Rev.
S. B. Gould, Curious Myths of the Middle Ages : Melusina.

[2] Fragments appended to Calmet's Dictionary of the Bible.

[3] Two Babylons, 445.

considers Oannês as equivalent to the Semitic
E-anush, or He-anesh, The Man. Enoush[1] signifies man as weak and mortal, as contrasted with
Eesh,[2] man valorous and powerful. This interpretation appears plausible, but by it the root
word On or Aun is lost. Oannês, too, has more
of the character of Eesh than of Enoush.[3] Mr.
Hislop's view may, however, be accepted as an
interpretation of one meaning of the name, if
Eanush be regarded as a Semitic transcription
of the Hamitic Oannês; explained by Professor
Rawlinson[4] as Hoa-Ana, i.e. the God Hoa. The
word Ana or Aun, here rendered 'god,' preserves
the root An or Aun; while the name Hoa or Ao,
as it is also rendered, appears exactly identical
with the Oë of Helladius. As to the meaning of
the name Hoa, Professor Rawlinson remarks:
'There are no means of strictly determining the
precise meaning of the word in Babylonian; but
it is perhaps allowable to connect it, provisionally,
with the Arabic Hiya, which is at once " life " and
a " serpent," since, according to Sir Henry Rawlinson, there are very strong grounds for connecting Hea or Hoa with the serpent of Scripture,

[1] Cf. Anthrôpos, Homo.   [2] Cf. Anêr, Vir.
[3] Enos, Gen. v. 6.   [4] Ancient Monarchies, i. 121.

I

and the Paradisaical traditions of the tree of knowledge and the tree of life.' [1]

SECTION XXXVIII.

NOAH AND OANNÊS.

THE parallel between Ôë or Oannês, the Chaldaean deity Hoa, and the patriarch Noah (Noa-h or n-Oa-h) is very remarkable ; and, despite of the sneers which have been bestowed in some quarters on the system of Euêmeros the Sikelian, who treated gods as deified mortals, I shall venture to apply Euêmeristic principles to the investigation of the history of these Dagonic personages. The great mistake generally committed in attempts to interpret Mythology is the natural error of stretching a particular theory or system beyond its proper limits, as if one key were sufficient to open all locks. The Natural Phenomena Theory, and the Euêmeristic Theory, are both admirably useful ; but, to ignore the merits of either, and, consequently, to depend wholly on the other, must necessarily be produc-

[1] Ancient Monarchies, i. 121.

tive of serious error in many instances. The
following are several of the points in the parallel
referred to : Oannês taught mankind the arts of
civilisation ; this, Noah, who survived the Flood
for several centuries, must necessarily have done ;
while Hoa is called the 'god of giving,' which is
explained by Bêrôsos as meaning that he was the
chief giver of gifts to man. The arts of sowing
and reaping were taught by Oannês, a circumstance which reminds us of Noah the Husbandman.
Oannês taught the use of letters and learning ;
Noah was necessarily a teacher ; and although
history is silent on the point, nothing is more
probable than that he should either have invented
or preserved the use of an alphabet or characters
of some kind. Xisuthros, the Noah of Chaldaean
legend, is said to have buried the sacred writings
before the Flood at Sippara, the Babylonian
Héliopolis, called Tsipar sha Shamas, Sippara of
the Sun (Shemesh), and mentioned in Scripture as
Sepharvaim or the Two Sipparas, there being one
on either side of the river,[1] and after the Flood
to have recovered them again ; while one of the
emblems of Hoa is the wedge or arrowhead, ' the
essential element of cuneiform writing.' Oannês,

[1] Ancient Monarchies, i. 15.   [2] Ib. i. 122.

although connected with the sea, is not a true sea-god or really marine divinity; so Noah's connection with the sea was only temporary, and the result of particular circumstances; and similarly, Professor Rawlinson remarks that Hoa is never called the 'lord of the sea,' which is the title of another Chaldaean deity, but on the contrary 'the lord of the earth,' which may have been a title of Noah, and which, at all events, must have expressed his position. Thus Oannês, Noah, and Poseidôn, are all equally Kings *in* the Sea, but not Kings *of* the Sea; a delicate point of agreement, and one which can scarcely have been purely accidental. Let it not, however, be hastily concluded from this comparison that I regard Poseidôn as absolutely representing Noah; I merely wish to point out the strong connection between the two. The life of Noah presents sufficient material to give rise to the conception of a score of deities; the cultus of each of whom might illustrate some aspect of the great patriarch's career, or develope some fresh traditional impression of his history. Damaskios (a Syrian of Damaskos), the last of the great Neo-Platonists, and who lived in the time of the Emperor Justinian, in his work entitled *Doubts and Solutions of the First Principles*, alludes to the god Hoa under the name of Aos

SECTION XXXIX.

POSEIDON AND HOA-ANA.

I TRUST it will not be thought that, in our wanderings Eastward, Poseidon has been left behind. In tracing the god through various countries and among different peoples, we meet with the personages Consus, Khons, Poseidon, Sidon, Dagon, Oän, Oannês, and Hoa-Ana. I have noticed the links that connect the three former; and it will be observed that their attribute of mysterious wisdom is one of the most striking characteristics of the three latter. Josephus states that the city of Sidon was named after the eldest son of Canaan, and such we may very reasonably suppose was the case; in the same way that Assyria received its name from Asshur, the deified son of Shem.[1] The name Sidon, in itself commemorative of the Flood, is just such an one as would be likely to have

[1] Rawlinson, Ancient Monarchies, ii. 3.

been bestowed by a grandson of Noah. The practical identity of the words Sidon and Dagon, and of the ideas expressed by them, will not, I think, be doubted; and this being accepted, it becomes impossible to separate Sidon from Poseidôn. With respect to the meaning of this word, the name of our great deity, Seidôn or Seidaon, appears clearly to signify the Ship of Aun, or of the Enlightening and Prolific Power. The first syllable of the name, Po, which is short, is more difficult to explain; and is, of course, the stronghold of those who believe in an Aryan Poseidôn, and who consequently treat it as the Greek root Po, which is connected with water and drinking. It is just possible that an Aryan first syllable may, for some reason, have been added to a Semitic name, either through error or otherwise; but it is probable that the apparent difficulty only arises from ignorance of the early Hamitic and Semitic forms of language. I have noticed [1] Gale's conjecture, that the name is derived from a Punic (Phoenician) word Pe-sitan, meaning 'expanse.' The god may truly be called the Wide-ruling, and the form Sitan sufficiently corresponds with

[1] Sec. xxxiv.

Sidon. Bailey[1] derives the name Poseidôn
'from the Phœnician word Posedoni, a breaker
or destroyer of ships.'[2] But this could never
have been the original meaning of the name,
for the god seems to have been always so called
among the Phœnicians, and the conception of
Poseidôn as a sea-god must have arisen prior to
that of Poseidôn as a Wrecker. However, whatever may be the exact force of the Pe or Po, the
question of the origin of the conception of the
god will be decided, not on the authority of a
doubtful syllable; but, in accordance with the
general catena of evidence, and on this I am
content to rest it. The connection between
Poseidôn, Sidon, and Dagon, being admitted, the
next point for consideration is the identity or
link between Dagon and Oannés. The evidence
in illustration of this is derived from ancient
writers, from a comparison of the forms and
characteristics of the two personages, and from
modern research in Chaldaea and Babylonia. I
noticed, in the legend of Oannés, that one of the
Oäns or Auns was called Ôdakôn (Ho Dagôn),
The Dag-Aun; and this Being has naturally

[1] Etymological English Dictionary, 1737, vol. ii.: Neptune.
[2] Cf. Od. xxiii. 234; xxiv. 109.

been identified with the Philistine and Phoenician Dagon. Again, the LXX. render Is. xlvi. 1 ' Bel (Bil-Nipru) boweth down, Dagôn (not Nebo) stoopeth.' They may be, and perhaps are, incorrect in their identification of Dagon and Nebo, although it may be observed that Nebo the Teacher and Instructor, god of writing, literature, and prophetic powers, has a resemblance in many points to Hoa-Ana, and may possibly be a reproduction of him; but it would be indeed remarkable if the LXX., living at such a comparatively short period after the overthrow of the Babylonian Empire, had introduced Dagon into the Chaldaean Pantheon without any authority and contrary to fact. The similarity of form and the corresponding characteristics of Dagon and Oannês are sufficiently evident, and have been already partially illustrated. Lastly, as regards modern research on the point, M. Oppert, and the French School generally, identify Bel with Dagon. Thus M. Lenormant observes —' Bel took many secondary forms, the most important being Bel-Dagon, a human bust springing from the body of a fish.' [1] But this identification is open to the two-fold objection,

---

[1] Ancient History of the East, i. 454.

(1) that it is entirely unsupported by history, *e.g.* the LXX. in the passage above quoted clearly distinguish between Bel and Dagon; and, (2) Bel or Bil was not a fish-god at all, either in Babylonia or Assyria. But, while the identity of Bel and Dagon may be safely rejected, the connection between Dagon and some god of the Chaldaean Pantheon is sufficiently evident, although Dagon, *eo nomine*, was probably unknown in Hamitic Chaldaea.[1] On the whole, every branch of the evidence points to the identity of Dagon and Oannês, which, I believe, is very generally accepted. Thus Mr. Cox observes—'By the Philistines, Oannes was worshipped under the name Dagon.'[2] The identity of Oannês with Hoa-Ana, I regard as being almost beyond dispute. But, Dagon having been identified with Poseidôn, this identification must be extended to Oannês or Hoa-Ana. This, however, does not imply that Hoa-Ana absolutely re-appears in the Greek Pantheon as Poseidôn; but merely that the ideas and belief which originally produced the conception of Hoa-Ana, in their gradual spread westward, produced

[1] Cf. Rawlinson, Ancient Monarchies. ii. 14.
[2] Manual of Mythology, 217.

other similar and derivative conceptions, amongst which Poseidôn is perhaps the most prominent. I will conclude this Section with a remark of Professor Rawlinson, an almost unrivalled authority on such a subject, which I particularly commend to the attention of the reader: 'Hoa occupies in the first [Chaldaean] Triad, *the position which in the classical mythology is filled by Poseidon,* and in some respects he corresponds to him. He is "the lord of the earth," just as Neptune [Poseidôn] is Gaiêochos.'[1] It will be observed that the Professor is not illustrating the connection between Hoa and Poseidôn, but merely remarks their strong mutual resemblance. That connection will, I trust, be considered to have been illustrated to some extent in the previous pages.

SECTION XL.

THE POSEIDÔN OF THE ORPHIC HYMNS.

THE supreme god in the Chaldaean Pantheon is Ra, a familiar Hamitic name applied also in

---

[1] *Ancient Monarchies,* i. 122; vide SS. xxvi. xxix.

Egypt to the Deity;[1] and the Semitic equivalent of which is Il, Ilu, El, Allah, Ilos, or Ilus. Below this source of deity stand a first Triad consisting of Ana or Anu, Anammelech,[2] *i.e.* Anu-Malik, the Aun-King of Sippara, Bil (Bel), and Hoa. From these elder gods descend or are produced all other divinities and mortals. Thus Bil is called 'the Father of the Gods,' while Hoa gives the 4,000 gods of heaven and earth the senses of seeing, hearing, and understanding. Hence, we can perceive why, in the Orphic Hymns, which present a faithful reflection of ancient ideas, Poseidôn is called 'the bringer of peace, health, and happiness (the gifts of Hoa), the ancient son of Zeus (*i.e.* Ra, or Il, the Supreme), the father of the blessed heavens, of gods, and men, who has obtained, second after Zeus, to reign over all.' This remarkable passage, ridiculously incorrect if applied only to the Homeric Poseidôn, becomes, when the god is traced to his origin, perfectly simple and comprehensible. Anu, the Aun, is said to represent 'the primordial chaos, the first material emanation of the divine being.'[3] This is in perfect

[1] Vide Sec. xxxvi.   [2] 2 Kings, xvii. 31.
[3] Lenormant, Ancient History of the East. i. 453.

harmony with the connection between Noah and
Oannês, for nothing is more natural than that
the idea of the pristine developing Chaos should
become confused with the subsequent progression
of life from the Ark-egg; or rather, perhaps,
that one personage should stand as a commemorative representation of both these facts.

SECTION XLI.

CONCLUSION.

THUS is the worship of Poseidôn traceable to its
source in the dim and distant East.   One and
yet many, ever changing in form yet preserving
the original ideas, we have marked its spread
from the starting point in Chaldaea, through
Phoenicia, Philistia, Libyé, and Greece.   Many
other lands, as Assyria, Arabia, and Asia Minor,
were doubtless equally subject to its sway.
Egypt, in some form, whether in the person of
Khons or otherwise, probably reproduced the
cultus; whilst Italy afforded it a home in the
West, and Phoenician enterprise would extend
its influence into the regions beyond.   There are

gods many and lords many; yet are they capable of being resolved into but few. So, some of the ancients believed that Osiris, Dionysos, Ploutôn, Jupiter, and other similar beings, were all in reality but one; and although the principle of identity may easily be incorrectly extended, yet in many instances one personage becomes manifold and multiform, as witness Hoa-Ana, Oannês, Onnes, Oän, Oë, Dagon, Sidon, and Poseidôn, the subject of our investigation. The materials from which Mythology is fabricated are the phenomena of the external world combined with the course of history, the ideas connected with the mystery of human existence and reproduction, the sense of religion (conscientiousness) implanted in the mind, and the feeling of fear or a realization of the capability of being injured. Thus man's Religious Mythology varies with the circumstances of his career, and with the scenery which surrounds him; whilst, in addition to these natural causes of difference, each of the three great branches of the Noachian Family preserve their distinct individuality and peculiar characteristics, all of which are more or less impressed upon the god whose progress I have attempted to trace. Poseidôn, in his journey westward, becomes by degrees more noble in conception and more innocent in cultus. His form, dropping the symbolical disguises that had enwrapped its earlier history, appears at length anthropomorphic, and consequently divine; and finally, when the golden coursers with their flowing manes have borne him in triumph in his eastern chariot to the stately home of Aigai, he is ready, as a fit companion, to join the Aryan divinities of Hellas; to sit with them in the halls of Olympos, second to none, save the great Overlord of All; and thus, to descend to all the Aftertime, as one of the foremost figures in that group of deities, the noblest and most beautiful ever imagined by the mind of man.

LONDON: PRINTED BY
SPOTTISWOODE AND CO., NEW-STREET SQUARE
AND PARLIAMENT STREET

GENERAL LIST OF WORKS

PUBLISHED BY

MESSRS. LONGMANS, GREEN, AND CO.

PATERNOSTER ROW, LONDON.

History, Politics, Historical Memoirs, &c.

The **HISTORY** of **ENGLAND** from the Fall of Wolsey to the Defeat of the Spanish Armada. By JAMES ANTHONY FROUDE. M.A. late Fellow of Exeter College, Oxford.
LIBRARY EDITION, 12 VOLS. 8vo. price £8 18s.
CABINET EDITION, In 12 vols. crown 8vo. price 72s.

The **HISTORY** of **ENGLAND** from the Accession of James II. By Lord MACAULAY.
STUDENT'S EDITION, 2 vols. crown 8vo. 12s.
PEOPLE'S EDITION, 4 vols. crown 8vo. 16s.
CABINET EDITION, 8 vols. post 8vo. 48s.
LIBRARY EDITION, 5 vols. 8vo. £4.

LORD MACAULAY'S WORKS. Complete and Uniform Library Edition. Edited by his Sister, Lady TREVELYAN. 8 vols. 8vo. with Portrait, price £5 5s. cloth, or £8 8s. bound in tree-calf by Rivière.

VARIETIES of **VICE-REGAL LIFE.** By Sir WILLIAM DENISON, K.C.B. late Governor-General of the Australian Colonies, and Governor of Madras. With Two Maps. 2 vols. 8vo. 28s.

On **PARLIAMENTARY GOVERNMENT** in **ENGLAND**: Its Origin, Development, and Practical Operation. By ALPHEUS TODD, Librarian of the Legislative Assembly of Canada. 2 vols. 8vo. price £1 17s.

A **HISTORICAL ACCOUNT** of the **NEUTRALITY** of **GREAT BRITAIN** DURING the AMERICAN CIVIL WAR. By MOUNTAGUE BERNARD, M.A. Chichele Professor of International Law and Diplomacy in the University of Oxford. Royal 8vo. 16s.

The **CONSTITUTIONAL HISTORY** of **ENGLAND**, since the Accession of George III. 1760—1860. By Sir THOMAS ERSKINE MAY, C.B. Second Edition. Cabinet Edition, thoroughly revised. 3 vols. crown 8vo. price 18s.

The **HISTORY** of **ENGLAND**, from the Earliest Times to the Year 1865. By C. D. YONGE, Regius Professor of Modern History in Queen's College, Belfast. New Edition. Crown 8vo. price 7s. 6d

A

The OXFORD REFORMERS—John Colet, Erasmus, and Thomas More; being a History of their Fellow-work. By FREDERIC SEEBOHM. Second Edition, enlarged. 8vo. 14s.

LECTURES on the HISTORY of ENGLAND, from the earliest Times to the Death of King Edward II. By WILLIAM LONGMAN. With Maps and Illustrations. 8vo. 15s.

The HISTORY of the LIFE and TIMES of EDWARD the THIRD. By WILLIAM LONGMAN. With 9 Maps, 3 Plates, and 16 Woodcuts. 2 vols. 8vo. 28s.

The OVERTHROW of the GERMANIC CONFEDERATION by PRUSSIA in 1866. By Sir ALEXANDER MALET, Bart. K.C.B. With 5 Maps. 8vo. 18s.

The MILITARY RESOURCES of PRUSSIA and FRANCE, and RECENT CHANGES in the ART of WAR. By Lieut.-Col. CHESNEY, R.E. and HENRY REEVE, D.C.L. Crown 8vo. price 7s. 6d.

WATERLOO LECTURES; a Study of the Campaign of 1815. By Colonel CHARLES C. CHESNEY, R.E. late Professor of Military Art and History in the Staff College. New Edition. 8vo. with Map, 10s. 6d.

DEMOCRACY in AMERICA. By ALEXIS DE TOCQUEVILLE. Translated by HENRY REEVE. 2 vols. 8vo. 21s.

HISTORY of the REFORMATION in EUROPE in the Time of Calvin. By J. H. MERLE D'AUBIGNÉ, D.D. Vols. I. and II. 8vo. 28s. VOL. III. 12s. VOL. IV. 16s. VOL. V. price 16s.

CHAPTERS from FRENCH HISTORY; St. Louis, Joan of Arc, Henri IV. with Sketches of the Intermediate Periods. By J. H. GURNEY, M.A. New Edition. Fcp. 8vo. 6s. 6d.

MEMOIR of POPE SIXTUS the FIFTH. By Baron HUBNER. Translated from the Original in French, with the Author's sanction, by HUBERT E. H. JERNINGHAM. 2 vols. 8vo. [In preparation.

IGNATIUS LOYOLA and the EARLY JESUITS. By STEWART ROSE. New Edition, revised. 8vo. with Portrait, price 16s.

The HISTORY of GREECE. By C. THIRLWALL, D.D. Lord Bishop of St. David's. 8 vols. fcp. 8vo. price 28s.

GREEK HISTORY from Themistocles to Alexander, in a Series of Lives from Plutarch. Revised and arranged by A. H. CLOUGH. New Edition. Fcp. with 44 Woodcuts, 6s.

CRITICAL HISTORY of the LANGUAGE and LITERATURE of Ancient Greece. By WILLIAM MURE, of Caldwell. 5 vols. 8vo. £3 9s.

The TALE of the GREAT PERSIAN WAR, from the Histories of Herodotus. By GEORGE W. COX, M.A. New Edition. Fcp. 3s. 6d.

HISTORY of the LITERATURE of ANCIENT GREECE. By Professor K. O. MULLER. Translated by the Right Hon. Sir GEORGE CORNEWALL LEWIS, Bart. and by J. W. DONALDSON, D.D. 3 vols. 8vo. 21s.

HISTORY of the CITY of ROME from its Foundation to the Sixteenth Century of the Christian Era. By THOMAS H. DYER, LLD. 8vo. with 2 Maps, 15s.

The HISTORY of ROME. By WILLIAM IHNE. English Edition, translated and revised by the Author. VOLS. I. and II. 8vo. price 30s.

HISTORY of the ROMANS under the EMPIRE. By the Very Rev. C. MERIVALE, D.C.L. Dean of Ely. 8 vols. post 8vo. 48s.

The FALL of the ROMAN REPUBLIC; a Short History of the Last Century of the Commonwealth. By the same Author. 12mo. 7s. 6d.

A STUDENT'S MANUAL of the HISTORY of INDIA, from the Earliest Period to the Present. By Colonel MEADOWS TAYLOR, M.R.A.S. M.R.I.A. Crown 8vo. with Maps, 7s. 6d.

The HISTORY of INDIA, from the Earliest Period to the close of Lord Dalhousie's Administration. By JOHN CLARK MARSHMAN. 3 vols. crown 8vo. 22s. 6d.

INDIAN POLITY: a View of the System of Administration in India. By Lieutenant-Colonel GEORGE CHESNEY, Fellow of the University of Calcutta. New Edition, revised; with Map. 8vo. price 21s.

HOME POLITICS; being a consideration of the Causes of the Growth of Trade in relation to Labour, Pauperism, and Emigration. By DANIEL GRANT. 8vo. 7s.

REALITIES of IRISH LIFE. By W. STEUART TRENCH, Land Agent in Ireland to the Marquess of Lansdowne, the Marquess of Bath, and Lord Digby. Fifth Edition. Crown 8vo. price 6s.

The STUDENT'S MANUAL of the HISTORY of IRELAND. By MARY F. CUSACK, Author of 'The Illustrated History of Ireland, from the Earliest Period to the Year of Catholic Emancipation.' Crown 8vo. price 6s.

CRITICAL and HISTORICAL ESSAYS contributed to the *Edinburgh Review.* By the Right Hon. LORD MACAULAY.

CABINET EDITION, 4 vols. post 8vo. 24s. | LIBRARY EDITION, 3 vols. 8vo. 36s.
PEOPLE'S EDITION, 2 vols. crown 8vo. 8s. | STUDENT'S EDITION, 1 vol. cr. 8vo. 6s.

SAINT-SIMON and SAINT-SIMONISM; a chapter in the History of Socialism in France. By ARTHUR J. BOOTH, M.A. Crown 8vo. price 7s. 6d.

HISTORY of EUROPEAN MORALS, from Augustus to Charlemagne. By W. E. H. LECKY, M.A. Second Edition. 2 vols. 8vo. price 28s.

HISTORY of the RISE and INFLUENCE of the SPIRIT of RATIONALISM in EUROPE. By W. E. H. LECKY, M.A. Cabinet Edition, being the Fourth. 2 vols. crown 8vo. price 16s.

GOD in HISTORY; or, the Progress of Man's Faith in the Moral Order of the World. By Baron BUNSEN. Translated by SUSANNA WINKWORTH; with a Preface by Dean STANLEY. 3 vols. 8vo. price 42s.

The HISTORY of PHILOSOPHY, from Thales to Comte. By GEORGE HENRY LEWES. Fourth Edition. 2 vols. 8vo. 32s.

An HISTORICAL VIEW of LITERATURE and ART in GREAT BRITAIN from the Accession of the House of Hanover to the Reign of Queen Victoria. By J. MURRAY GRAHAM, M.A. 8vo. price 14s.

The MYTHOLOGY of the ARYAN NATIONS. By GEORGE W. COX, M.A. late Scholar of Trinity College, Oxford, Joint-Editor, with the late Professor Brande, of the Fourth Edition of 'The Dictionary of Science, Literature, and Art.' Author of 'Tales of Ancient Greece,' &c. 2 vols. 8vo. 28s.

HISTORY of CIVILISATION in England and France, Spain and Scotland. By HENRY THOMAS BUCKLE. New Edition of the entire Work with a complete INDEX. 3 vols. crown 8vo. 24s.

HISTORY of the CHRISTIAN CHURCH, from the Ascension of Christ to the Conversion of Constantine. By E. BURTON, D.D. late Prof. of Divinity in the Univ. of Oxford. New Edition. Fcp. 3s. 6d.

SKETCH of the HISTORY of the CHURCH of ENGLAND to the Revolution of 1688. By the Right Rev. T. V. SHORT, D.D. Lord Bishop of St. Asaph. Eighth Edition. Crown 8vo. 7s. 6d.

HISTORY of the EARLY CHURCH, from the First Preaching of the Gospel to the Council of Nicæa. A.D. 325. By ELIZABETH M. SEWELL, Author of 'Amy Herbert.' New Edition, with Questions. Fcp. 4s. 6d.

The ENGLISH REFORMATION. By F. C. MASSINGBERD, M.A. Chancellor of Lincoln and Rector of South Ormsby. Fourth Edition, revised. Fcp. 8vo. 7s. 6d.

MAUNDER'S HISTORICAL TREASURY; comprising a General Introductory Outline of Universal History, and a series of Separate Histories. Latest Edition, revised and brought down to the Present Time by the Rev. GEORGE WILLIAM COX, M.A. Fcp. 6s. cloth, or 9s. 6d. calf.

HISTORICAL and CHRONOLOGICAL ENCYCLOPÆDIA; comprising Chronological Notices of all the Great Events of Universal History: Treaties, Alliances, Wars, Battles, &c.; Incidents in the Lives of Eminent Men and their Works, Scientific and Geographical Discoveries, Mechanical Inventions, and Social, Domestic, and Economical Improvements. By B. B. WOODWARD, B.A. and W. L. R. CATES. 1 vol. 8vo.   [In the press.

Biographical Works.

A MEMOIR of DANIEL MACLISE, R.A. By W. JUSTIN O'DRISCOLL, M.R.I.A. Barrister-at-Law. With Portrait and Woodcuts. Post 8vo. price 7s. 6d.

MEMOIRS of the MARQUIS of POMBAL; with Extracts from his Writings and from Despatches in the State Papers Office. By the CONDE DA CARNOTA. New Edition. 8vo. price 7s.

REMINISCENCES of FIFTY YEARS. By MARK BOYD. Post 8vo. price 10s. 6d.

The LIFE of ISAMBARD KINGDOM BRUNEL, Civil Engineer. By ISAMBARD BRUNEL, B.C.L. of Lincoln's Inn; Chancellor of the Diocese of Ely. With Portrait, Plates, and Woodcuts. 8vo. 21s.

The LIFE and LETTERS of FARADAY. By Dr. BENCE JONES, Secretary of the Royal Institution. Second Edition, thoroughly revised. 2 vols. 8vo. with Portrait, and Eight Engravings on Wood, price 28s.

FARADAY as a DISCOVERER. By JOHN TYNDALL, LL.D. F.R.S. Professor of Natural Philosophy in the Royal Institution. New and Cheaper Edition, with Two Portraits. Fcp. 8vo. 3s. 6d.

The LIFE and LETTERS of the Rev. SYDNEY SMITH. Edited by his Daughter, Lady HOLLAND, and Mrs. AUSTIN. New Edition, complete in One Volume. Crown 8vo. price 6s.

SOME MEMORIALS of R. D. HAMPDEN, Bishop of Hereford. Edited by his Daughter, HENRIETTA HAMPDEN. With Portrait. 8vo. price 12s.

The LIFE and TRAVELS of GEORGE WHITEFIELD, M.A.   By
JAMES PATERSON GLEDSTONE.   8vo. price 14s.

LIVES of the LORD CHANCELLORS and KEEPERS of the GREAT
SEAL of IRELAND, from the Earliest Times to the Reign of Queen
Victoria. By J. R. O'FLANAGAN, M.R.I.A. Barrister-at-Law.   2 vols. 8vo. 36s.

DICTIONARY of GENERAL BIOGRAPHY; containing Concise
Memoirs and Notices of the most Eminent Persons of all Countries, from
the Earliest Ages to the Present Time. Edited by W. L. R. CATES.   8vo. 21s.

LIVES of the QUEENS of ENGLAND.   By AGNES STRICKLAND.
Library Edition, newly revised; with Portraits of every Queen, Autographs,
and Vignettes.   8 vols. post 8vo. 7s. 6d. each.

LIFE of the DUKE of WELLINGTON.   By the Rev. G. R. GLEIG,
M.A.   Popular Edition, carefully revised; with copious Additions.   Crown
8vo. with Portrait, 5s.

HISTORY of MY RELIGIOUS OPINIONS. By J. H. NEWMAN, D.D.
Being the Substance of Apologia pro Vitâ Suâ.   Post 8vo. 6s.

The PONTIFICATE of PIUS the NINTH; being the Third Edition
of 'Rome and its Ruler,' continued to the latest moment and greatly
enlarged.   By J. F. MAGUIRE, M.P.   Post 8vo. with Portrait, 12s. 6d.

FATHER MATHEW: a Biography.   By JOHN FRANCIS MAGUIRE,
M.P. for Cork.   Popular Edition, with Portrait.   Crown 8vo. 3s. 6d.

FELIX MENDELSSOHN'S LETTERS from *Italy and Switzerland*,
and *Letters from* 1833 *to* 1847, translated by Lady WALLACE.   New Edition,
with Portrait.   2 vols. crown 8vo. 5s. each.

MEMOIRS of SIR HENRY HAVELOCK, K.C.B.   By JOHN CLARK
MARSHMAN.   Cabinet Edition, with Portrait.   Crown 8vo. price 3s. 6d.

VICISSITUDES of FAMILIES.   By Sir J. BERNARD BURKE, C.B.
Ulster King of Arms.   New Edition, remodelled and enlarged.   2 vols.
crown 8vo. 21s.

ESSAYS in ECCLESIASTICAL BIOGRAPHY.   By the Right Hon.
Sir J. STEPHEN, LL.D.   Cabinet Edition, being the Fifth.   Crown 8vo. 7s. 6d.

MAUNDER'S BIOGRAPHICAL TREASURY.   Thirteenth Edition,
reconstructed, thoroughly revised, and in great part rewritten; with about
1,000 additional Memoirs and Notices, by W. L. R. CATES.   Fcp. 6s.

LETTERS and LIFE of FRANCIS BACON, including all his Occa-
sional Works.   Collected and edited, with a Commentary, by J. SPEDDING,
Trin. Coll. Cantab.   VOLS. I. and II. 8vo. 24s.   VOLS. III. and IV. 24s.
VOL. V. price 12s.

Criticism, Philosophy, Polity, &c.

The INSTITUTES of JUSTINIAN; with English Introduction, Translation, and Notes.   By T. C. SANDARS, M.A. Barrister, late Fellow of Oriel
Coll. Oxon.   New Edition.   8vo. 15s.

SOCRATES and the **SOCRATIC SCHOOLS.** Translated from the German of Dr. E. ZELLER, with the Author's approval, by the Rev. OSWALD J. REICHEL, B.C.L. and M.A. Crown 8vo. 8s. 6d.

The STOICS, EPICUREANS, and SCEPTICS. Translated from the German of Dr. E. ZELLER, with the Author's approval, by OSWALD J. REICHEL, B.C.L. and M.A. Crown 8vo. price 14s.

The ETHICS of ARISTOTLE, illustrated with Essays and Notes. By Sir A. GRANT, Bart. M.A. LL.D. Second Edition, revised and completed. 2 vols. 8vo. price 28s.

The NICOMACHEAN ETHICS of ARISTOTLE newly translated into English. By R. WILLIAMS, B.A. Fellow and late Lecturer of Merton College, and sometime Student of Christ Church, Oxford. 8vo. 12s.

ELEMENTS of LOGIC. By R. WHATELY, D.D. late Archbishop of Dublin. New Edition. 8vo. 10s. 6d. crown 8vo. 4s. 6d.

Elements of Rhetoric. By the same Author. New Edition. 8vo. 10s. 8d. crown 8vo. 4s. 6d.

English Synonymes. By E. JANE WHATELY. Edited by Archbishop WHATELY. 5th Edition. Fcp. 3s.

BACON'S ESSAYS with **ANNOTATIONS.** By R. WHATELY, D.D. late Archbishop of Dublin. Sixth Edition. 8vo. 10s. 6d.

LORD BACON'S WORKS, collected and edited by J. SPEDDING, M.A. R. L. ELLIS, M.A. and D. D. HEATH. New and Cheaper Edition. 7 vols. 8vo. price £3 13s. 6d.

The SUBJECTION of WOMEN. By JOHN STUART MILL. New Edition. Post 8vo. 5s.

On REPRESENTATIVE GOVERNMENT. By JOHN STUART MILL. Third Edition. 8vo. 9s. Crown 8vo. 2s.

On LIBERTY. By JOHN STUART MILL. Fourth Edition. Post 8vo. 7s. 6d. Crown 8vo. 1s. 4d.

PRINCIPLES of POLITICAL ECONOMY. By the same Author. Eighth Edition. 2 vols. 8vo. 30s. Or in 1 vol. crown 8vo. 5s.

A SYSTEM of LOGIC, RATIOCINATIVE and INDUCTIVE. By the same Author. Seventh Edition. Two vols. 8vo. 25s.

ANALYSIS of Mr. MILL'S SYSTEM of LOGIC. By W. STEBBING, M.A. Fellow of Worcester College, Oxford. New Edition. 12mo. 3s. 6d.

UTILITARIANISM. By JOHN STUART MILL. Fourth Edition. 8vo. 5s.

DISSERTATIONS and DISCUSSIONS, POLITICAL, PHILOSOPHI-CAL, and HISTORICAL. By JOHN STUART MILL. Second Edition, revised. 3 vols. 8vo. 36s.

EXAMINATION of Sir W. HAMILTON'S PHILOSOPHY, and of the Principal Philosophical Questions discussed in his Writings. By JOHN STUART MILL. Third Edition. 8vo. 16s.

An OUTLINE of the NECESSARY LAWS of THOUGHT: a Treatise on Pure and Applied Logic. By the Most Rev. WILLIAM, Lord Arch-bishop of York, D.D. F.R.S. Ninth Thousand. Crown 8vo. 5s. 6d.

The ELEMENTS of POLITICAL ECONOMY. By HENRY DUNNING MACLEOD, M.A. Barrister-at-Law. 8vo. 16s.

A Dictionary of Political Economy; Biographical, Bibliographical, Historical, and Practical. By the same Author. VOL. I. royal 8vo. 32s.

The ELECTION of REPRESENTATIVES, Parliamentary and Municipal; a Treatise. By THOMAS HARE, Barrister-at-Law. Third Edition, with Additions. Crown 8vo. 6s.

SPEECHES of the RIGHT HON. LORD MACAULAY, corrected by Himself. People's Edition, crown 8vo. 3s. 6d.

Lord Macaulay's Speeches on Parliamentary Reform in 1831 and 1832. 18mo. 1s.

INAUGURAL ADDRESS delivered to the University of St. Andrews. By JOHN STUART MILL. 8vo. 5s. People's Edition, crown 8vo. 1s.

A DICTIONARY of the ENGLISH LANGUAGE. By R. G. LATHAM, M.A. M.D. F.R.S. Founded on the Dictionary of Dr. SAMUEL JOHNSON, as edited by the Rev. H. J. TODD, with numerous Emendations and Additions. In Four Volumes, 4to. price £7.

THESAURUS of ENGLISH WORDS and PHRASES, classified and arranged so as to facilitate the Expression of Ideas, and assist in Literary Composition. By P. M. ROGET, M.D. New Edition. Crown 8vo. 10s. 6d.

LECTURES on the SCIENCE of LANGUAGE. By F. MAX MÜLLER, M.A. &c. Foreign Member of the French Institute. Sixth Edition. 2 vols. crown 8vo. price 16s.

CHAPTERS on LANGUAGE. By FREDERIC W. FARRAR, F.R.S. Head Master of Marlborough College. Crown 8vo. 8s. 6d.

The DEBATER; a Series of Complete Debates, Outlines of Debates, and Questions for Discussion. By F. ROWTON. Fcp. 6s.

MANUAL of ENGLISH LITERATURE, Historical and Critical. By THOMAS ARNOLD, M.A. Second Edition. Crown 8vo. price 7s. 6d.

SOUTHEY'S DOCTOR, complete in One Volume. Edited by the Rev. J. W. WARTER, B.D. Square crown 8vo. 12s. 6d.

HISTORICAL and CRITICAL COMMENTARY on the OLD TESTAMENT; with a New Translation. By M. M. KALISCH, Ph.D. VOL. I. Genesis, 8vo. 18s. or adapted for the General Reader, 12s. VOL. II. Exodus, 15s. or adapted for the General Reader, 12s. VOL. III. Leviticus, PART I. 15s. or adapted for the General Reader, 8s.

A HEBREW GRAMMAR, with EXERCISES. By M. M. KALISCH, Ph.D. PART I. Outlines with Exercises, 8vo. 12s. 6d. KEY. 5s. PART II. Exceptional Forms and Constructions, 12s. 6d.

A LATIN-ENGLISH DICTIONARY. By JOHN T. WHITE, D.D. Oxon. and J. E. RIDDLE, M.A. Oxon. Third Edition, revised. 2 vols. 4to. pp. 2,128. price 42s. cloth.

White's College Latin-English Dictionary (Intermediate Size), abridged for the use of University Students from the Parent Work (as above). Medium 8vo. pp. 1,048, price 18s. cloth.

White's Junior Student's Complete Latin-English and English-Latin Dictionary. New Edition. Square 12mo. pp. 1,058, price 12s.

Separately { The ENGLISH-LATIN DICTIONARY, price 5s. 6d.
The LATIN-ENGLISH DICTIONARY, price 7s. 6d.

An **ENGLISH-GREEK LEXICON**, containing all the Greek Words used by Writers of good authority. By C. D. YONGE, B.A. New Edition. 4to. 21s.

Mr. YONGE'S NEW LEXICON, English and Greek, abridged from his larger work (as above). Revised Edition. Square 12mo. 8s. 6d.

A **GREEK-ENGLISH LEXICON**. Compiled by H. G. LIDDELL, D.D. Dean of Christ Church, and R. SCOTT, D.D. Dean of Rochester. Sixth Edition. Crown 4to. price 36s.

A Lexicon, Greek and English, abridged from LIDDELL and SCOTT's *Greek-English Lexicon*. Twelfth Edition. Square 12mo. 7s. 6d.

A **SANSKRIT-ENGLISH DICTIONARY**, the Sanskrit words printed both in the original Devanagari and in Roman Letters. Compiled by T. BENFEY, Prof. in the Univ. of Göttingen. 8vo. 52s. 6d.

WALKER'S PRONOUNCING DICTIONARY of the **ENGLISH LANGUAGE**. Thoroughly revised Editions, by B. H. SMART. 8vo. 12s. 16mo. 6s.

A **PRACTICAL DICTIONARY** of the **FRENCH** and **ENGLISH LANGUAGES**. By L. CONTANSEAU. Fourteenth Edition. Post 8vo. 10s. 6d.

Contanseau's Pocket Dictionary, French and English, abridged from the above by the Author. New Edition, revised. Square 18mo. 3s. 6d.

NEW PRACTICAL DICTIONARY of the **GERMAN LANGUAGE**; German-English and English-German. By the Rev. W. L. BLACKLEY, M.A. and Dr. CARL MARTIN FRIEDLÄNDER. Post 8vo. 7s. 6d.

The **MASTERY of LANGUAGES**; or, the Art of Speaking Foreign Tongues Idiomatically. By THOMAS PRENDERGAST, late of the Civil Service at Madras. Second Edition. 8vo. 6s.

Miscellaneous Works and Popular Metaphysics.

The **ESSAYS and CONTRIBUTIONS** of A. K. H. B., Author of ' The Recreations of a Country Parson.' Uniform Editions:—

Recreations of a Country Parson. By A. K. H. B. FIRST and SECOND SERIES, crown 8vo. 3s. 6d. each.

The **COMMON-PLACE PHILOSOPHER** in TOWN and COUNTRY. By A. K. H. B. Crown 8vo. price 3s. 6d.

Leisure Hours in Town; Essays Consolatory, Æsthetical, Moral, Social, and Domestic. By A. K. H. B. Crown 8vo. 3s. 6d.

The Autumn Holidays of a Country Parson; Essays contributed to *Fraser's Magazine* and to *Good Words*. By A. K. H. B. Crown 8vo. 3s. 6d.

The **Graver Thoughts** of a Country Parson. By A. K. H. B. FIRST and SECOND SERIES, crown 8vo. 3s. 6d. each.

Critical Essays of a Country Parson, selected from Essays contributed to *Fraser's Magazine*. By A. K. H. B. Crown 8vo. 3s. 6d.

Sunday Afternoons at the Parish Church of a Scottish University City. By A. K. H. B. Crown 8vo. 3s. 6d.

LESSONS of MIDDLE AGE; with some Account of various Cities and Men. By A. K. H. B. Crown 8vo. 3s. 6d.

Counsel and Comfort spoken from a City Pulpit. By A. K. H. B. Crown 8vo. price 3s. 6d.

Changed Aspects of Unchanged Truths; Memorials of St. Andrews Sundays. By A. K. H.B. Crown 8vo. 3s. 6d.

Present-day Thoughts; Memorials of St. Andrews Sundays. By A. K. H. B. Crown 8vo. 3s. 6d.

SHORT STUDIES on GREAT SUBJECTS. By JAMES ANTHONY FROUDE. M.A. late Fellow of Exeter Coll. Oxford. Third Edition. 8vo. 12s. SECOND SERIES. 8vo. price 12s.

LORD MACAULAY'S MISCELLANEOUS WRITINGS :—
LIBRARY EDITION. 2 vols. 8vo. Portrait, 21s.
PEOPLE'S EDITION. 1 vol. crown 8vo. 4s. 6d.

LORD MACAULAY'S MISCELLANEOUS WRITINGS and SPEECHES.
STUDENT'S EDITION, in crown 8vo. price 6s.

The REV. SYDNEY SMITH'S MISCELLANEOUS WORKS; including his Contributions to the *Edinburgh Review*. Crown 8vo. 6s.

The Wit and Wisdom of the Rev. Sydney Smith; a Selection of the most memorable Passages in his Writings and Conversation. 16mo. 3s. 6d.

The ECLIPSE of FAITH; or, a Visit to a Religious Sceptic. By HENRY ROGERS. Twelfth Edition. Fcp. 5s.

Defence of the Eclipse of Faith, by its Author; a rejoinder to Dr. Newman's *Reply*. Third Edition. Fcp. 3s. 6d.

Selections from the Correspondence of R. E. H. Greyson. By the same Author. Third Edition. Crown 8vo. 7s. 6d.

FAMILIES of SPEECH. Four Lectures delivered at the Royal Institution of Great Britain. By the Rev. F. W. FARRAR, M.A. F.R.S. Head Master of Marlborough College. Post 8vo. with Two Maps, 5s. 6d.

CHIPS from a GERMAN WORKSHOP; being Essays on the Science of Religion, and on Mythology, Traditions, and Customs. By F. MAX MÜLLER, M.A. &c. Foreign Member of the French Institute. 3 vols. 8vo. £2.

UEBERWEG'S SYSTEM of LOGIC and HISTORY of LOGICAL DOCTRINES. Translated, with Notes and Appendices, by T. M. LINDSAY, M.A. F.R.S.E. Examiner in Philosophy to the University of Edinburgh. 8vo. price 16s.

ANALYSIS of the PHENOMENA of the HUMAN MIND. By JAMES MILL. A New Edition, with Notes, Illustrative and Critical, by ALEXANDER BAIN, ANDREW FINDLATER, and GEORGE GROTE. Edited, with additional Notes, by JOHN STUART MILL. 2 vols. 8vo. price 28s.

An INTRODUCTION to MENTAL PHILOSOPHY, on the Inductive Method. By J. D. MORELL, M.A. LL.D. 8vo. 12s.

ELEMENTS of PSYCHOLOGY, containing the Analysis of the Intellectual Powers. By the same Author. Post 8vo. 7s. 6d.

The SECRET of HEGEL: being the Hegelian System in Origin, Principle, Form, and Matter. By J. H. STIRLING. 2 vols. 8vo. 28s.

SIR WILLIAM HAMILTON; being the Philosophy of Perception: an Analysis. By J. H. STIRLING. 8vo. 5s.

The SENSES and the INTELLECT. By ALEXANDER BAIN, M.D. Professor of Logic in the University of Aberdeen. Third Edition. 8vo. 15s.

MENTAL and MORAL SCIENCE: a Compendium of Psychology and Ethics. By the same Author. Second Edition. Crown 8vo. 10s. 6d.

LOGIC, DEDUCTIVE and INDUCTIVE. By the same Author. In Two PARTS, crown 8vo. 10s. 6d. Each Part may be had separately:—
PART I. Deduction, 4s. PART II. Induction, 6s. 6d.

TIME and SPACE; a Metaphysical Essay. By SHADWORTH H. HODGSON. (This work covers the whole ground of Speculative Philosophy.) 8vo. price 16s.

The Theory of Practice; an Ethical Inquiry. By the same Author. (This work, in conjunction with the foregoing, completes a system of Philosophy.) 2 vols. 8vo. price 24s.

The PHILOSOPHY of NECESSITY; or, Natural Law as applicable to Mental, Moral, and Social Science. By CHARLES BRAY. Second Edition. 8vo. 9s.

The Education of the Feelings and Affections. By the same Author. Third Edition. 8vo. 3s. 6d.

On Force, its Mental and Moral Correlates. By the same Author. 8vo. 5s.

A TREATISE on HUMAN NATURE; being an Attempt to Introduce the Experimental Method of Reasoning into Moral Subjects. By DAVID HUME. Edited, with Notes, &c. by T. H. GREEN, Fellow, and T. H. GROSE, late Scholar, of Balliol College, Oxford.   [In the press.

ESSAYS MORAL, POLITICAL, and LITERARY. By DAVID HUME. By the same Editors.   [In the press.

Astronomy, Meteorology, Popular Geography, &c.

OUTLINES of ASTRONOMY. By Sir J. F. W. HERSCHEL, Bart. Eleventh Edition, with Plates and Woodcuts. Square crown 8vo. 12s.

The SUN; RULER, LIGHT, FIRE, and LIFE of the PLANETARY SYSTEM. By RICHARD A. PROCTOR, B.A. F.R.A.S. With 10 Plates (7 coloured) and 107 Figures on Wood. Crown 8vo. 14s.

OTHER WORLDS THAN OURS; the Plurality of Worlds Studied under the Light of Recent Scientific Researches. By the same Author. Second Edition, with 14 Illustrations. Crown 8vo. 10s. 6d.

SATURN and its SYSTEM. By the same Author. 8vo. with 14 Plates, 14s.

SCHELLEN'S SPECTRUM ANALYSIS, in its application to Terrestrial Substances and the Physical Constitution of the Heavenly Bodies. Translated by JANE and C. LASSELL; edited by W. HUGGINS, LL.D. F.R.S. Crown 8vo. with Illustrations.   [Nearly ready.

CELESTIAL OBJECTS for **COMMON TELESCOPES.** By the Rev. T. W. WEBB, M.A. F.R.A.S. Second Edition, revised, with a large Map of the Moon, and several Woodcuts. 16mo. 7s. 6d.

NAVIGATION and **NAUTICAL ASTRONOMY** (Practical, Theoretical, Scientific) for the use of Students and Practical Men. By J. MERRIFIELD, F.R.A.S and H. EVERS. 8vo. 14s.

DOVE'S LAW of **STORMS,** considered in connexion with the Ordinary Movements of the Atmosphere. Translated by R. H. SCOTT, M.A. T.C.D. 8vo. 10s. 6d.

The **CANADIAN DOMINION.** By CHARLES MARSHALL. With 6 Illustrations on Wood. 8vo. price 12s. 6d.

A **GENERAL DICTIONARY** of **GEOGRAPHY,** Descriptive, Physical, Statistical, and Historical: forming a complete Gazetteer of the World. By A. KEITH JOHNSTON, LL.D. F.R.G.S. Revised Edition. 8vo. 31s. 6d.

A **MANUAL** of **GEOGRAPHY,** Physical, Industrial, and Political. By W. HUGHES, F.R.G.S. With 6 Maps. Fcp. 7s. 6d.

MAUNDER'S TREASURY of **GEOGRAPHY,** Physical, Historical, Descriptive, and Political. Edited by W. HUGHES, F.R.G.S. Revised Edition, with 7 Maps and 16 Plates. Fcp. 6s. cloth, or 9s. 6d. bound in calf.

The **PUBLIC SCHOOLS ATLAS** of **MODERN GEOGRAPHY.** In 31 Maps, exhibiting clearly the more important Physical Features of the Countries delineated, and Noting all the Chief Places of Historical, Commercial, or Social Interest. Edited, with an Introduction, by the Rev. G. BUTLER, M.A. Imp. 4to. price 3s. 6d. sewed, or 5s. cloth. [Nearly ready.

Natural History and Popular Science.

ELEMENTARY TREATISE on **PHYSICS,** Experimental and Applied. Translated and edited from GANOT's Eléments de Physique (with the Author's sanction) by E. ATKINSON, Ph.D. F.C.S. New Edition, revised and enlarged; with a Coloured Plate and 620 Woodcuts. Post 8vo. 15s.

The **ELEMENTS** of **PHYSICS** or **NATURAL PHILOSOPHY.** By NEIL ARNOTT, M.D. F.R.S. Physician Extraordinary to the Queen. Sixth Edition, rewritten and completed. Two Parts. 8vo. 21s.

SOUND: a Course of Eight Lectures delivered at the Royal Institution of Great Britain. By JOHN TYNDALL, LL.D. F.R.S. New Edition, crown 8vo. with Portrait of M. Chladni and 169 Woodcuts, price 9s.

HEAT a MODE of **MOTION.** By Professor JOHN TYNDALL, LL.D. F.R.S. Fourth Edition, Crown 8vo. with Woodcuts, 10s. 6d.

RESEARCHES on **DIAMAGNETISM** and **MAGNE-CRYSTALLIC ACTION**; including the Question of Diamagnetic Polarity. By the same Author. With 6 Plates and many Woodcuts. 8vo. price 14s.

PROFESSOR TYNDALL'S ESSAYS on the **USE** and **LIMIT** of the **IMAGINATION** in SCIENCE. Being the Second Edition, with Additions, of his Discourse on the Scientific Use of the Imagination. 8vo. 3s.,

NOTES of a COURSE of SEVEN LECTURES on ELECTRICAL PHENOMENA and THEORIES, delivered at the Royal Institution, A.D. 1870. By Professor TYNDALL. Crown 8vo. 1s. sewed, or 1s. 6d. cloth.

NOTES of a COURSE of NINE LECTURES on LIGHT delivered at the Royal Institution, A.D. 1869. By the same Author. Crown 8vo. price 1s. sewed, or 1s. 6d. cloth.

FRAGMENTS of SCIENCE for UNSCIENTIFIC PEOPLE; a Series of detached Essays, Lectures, and Reviews. By JOHN TYNDALL, LL.D. F.R.S. Second Edition. 8vo. price 14s.

LIGHT SCIENCE for LEISURE HOURS; a Series of Familiar Essays on Scientific Subjects, Natural Phenomena, &c. By R. A. PROCTOR, B.A. F.R.A.S. Crown 8vo. price 7s. 6d.

LIGHT: Its Influence on Life and Health. By FORBES WINSLOW, M.D. D.C.L. Oxon. (Hon.). Fcp. 8vo. 6s.

A TREATISE on ELECTRICITY, in Theory and Practice. By A. DE LA RIVE, Prof. in the Academy of Geneva. Translated by C. V. WALKER, F.R.S. 3 vols. 8vo. with Woodcuts, £3 13s.

The BEGINNING: its When and its How. By MUNGO PONTON, F.R.S.E. Post 8vo. with very numerous Illustrations, price 18s.

The CORRELATION of PHYSICAL FORCES. By W. R. GROVE, Q.C. V.P.R.S. Fifth Edition, revised, and followed by a Discourse on Continuity. 8vo. 10s. 6d. The *Discourse on Continuity*, separately, 2s. 6d.

MANUAL of GEOLOGY. By S. HAUGHTON, M.D. F.R.S. Revised Edition, with 66 Woodcuts. Fcp. 7s. 6d.

VAN DER HOEVEN'S HANDBOOK of ZOOLOGY. Translated from the Second Dutch Edition by the Rev. W. CLARK, M.D. F.R.S. 2 vols. 8vo. with 24 Plates of Figures, 60s.

Professor OWEN'S LECTURES on the COMPARATIVE ANATOMY and Physiology of the Invertebrate Animals. Second Edition, with 235 Woodcuts. 8vo. 21s.

The COMPARATIVE ANATOMY and PHYSIOLOGY of the VERTE-brate Animals. By RICHARD OWEN, F.R.S. D.C.L. With 1,472 Woodcuts. 3 vols. 8vo. £3 13s. 6d.

The ORIGIN of CIVILISATION and the PRIMITIVE CONDITION of MAN; Mental and Social Condition of Savages. By Sir JOHN LUBBOCK, Bart. M.P. F.R.S. Second Edition, with 25 Woodcuts. 8vo. price 16s.

The PRIMITIVE INHABITANTS of SCANDINAVIA: containing a Description of the Implements, Dwellings, Tombs, and Mode of Living of the Savages in the North of Europe during the Stone Age. By SVEN NILSSON. With 16 Plates of Figures and 3 Woodcuts. 8vo. 18s.

BIBLE ANIMALS; being a Description of every Living Creature mentioned in the Scriptures, from the Ape to the Coral. By the Rev. J. G. WOOD, M.A. F.L.S. With about 100 Vignettes on Wood. 8vo. 21s.

HOMES WITHOUT HANDS: a Description of the Habitations of Animals, classed according to their Principle of Construction. By Rev. J. G. WOOD, M.A. F.L.S. With about 140 Vignettes on Wood. 8vo. 21s.

INSECTS AT HOME. By the Rev. J. G. WOOD, M.A. F.L.S. With a Frontispiece in Colours, 21 full-page Illustrations, and about 700 smaller Illustrations from original designs engraved on Wood by G. Pearson. 8vo. price 21s.

STRANGE DWELLINGS; being a description of the Habitations of Animals, abridged from ' Homes without Hands.' By J. G. WOOD, M.A. F.L.S. With a New Frontispiece and about 60 other Woodcut Illustrations. Crown 8vo. price 7s. 6d.

A FAMILIAR HISTORY of BIRDS. By E. STANLEY, D.D. F.R.S. late Lord Bishop of Norwich. Seventh Edition, with Woodcuts. Fcp. 3s. 6d.

The **HARMONIES of NATURE and UNITY of CREATION.** By Dr. GEORGE HARTWIG. 8vo. with numerous Illustrations, 18s.

The **SEA and its LIVING WONDERS.** By the same Author. Third (English) Edition. 8vo. with many Illustrations, 21s.

The **TROPICAL WORLD.** By Dr. GEO. HARTWIG. With 8 Chromo-xylographs and 172 Woodcuts. 8vo. 21s.

The **SUBTERRANEAN WORLD.** By Dr. GEORGE HARTWIG. With 3 Maps and about 80 Woodcuts, including 8 full size of page. 8vo. price 21s.

The **POLAR WORLD**, a Popular Description of Man and Nature in the Arctic and Antarctic Regions of the Globe. By Dr. GEORGE HARTWIG. With 8 Chromoxylographs, 3 Maps, and 85 Woodcuts. 8vo. 21s.

KIRBY and **SPENCE'S INTRODUCTION to ENTOMOLOGY**, or Elements of the Natural History of Insects. 7th Edition. Crown 8vo. 5s.

MAUNDER'S TREASURY of NATURAL HISTORY, or Popular Dictionary of Zoology. Revised and corrected by T. S. COBBOLD, M.D. Fcp. with 900 Woodcuts, 6s. cloth, or 9s. 6d. bound in calf.

The **TREASURY of BOTANY**, or Popular Dictionary of the Vegetable Kingdom; including a Glossary of Botanical Terms. Edited by J. LINDLEY, F.R.S. and T. MOORE, F.L.S. assisted by eminent Contributors. With 274 Woodcuts and 20 Steel Plates. Two Parts, fcp. 12s. cloth, or 19s. calf.

The **ELEMENTS of BOTANY** for **FAMILIES and SCHOOLS.** Tenth Edition, revised by THOMAS MOORE, F.L.S. Fcp. with 154 Woodcuts. 2s. 6d.

The **ROSE AMATEUR'S GUIDE.** By THOMAS RIVERS. Ninth Edition. Fcp. 4s.

LOUDON'S ENCYCLOPÆDIA of PLANTS; comprising the Specific Character, Description, Culture, History, &c. of all the Plants found in Great Britain. With upwards of 12,000 Woodcuts. 8vo. 42s.

MAUNDER'S SCIENTIFIC and LITERARY TREASURY. New Edition, thoroughly revised and in great part re-written, with above 1,000 new Articles, by J. Y. JOHNSON, Corr. M.Z.S. Fcp. 6s. cloth, or 9s. 6d. calf.

A DICTIONARY of SCIENCE, LITERATURE, and ART. Fourth Edition, re-edited by W. T. BRANDE (the original Author), and GEORGE W. COX, M.A. assisted by contributors of eminent Scientific and Literary Acquirements. 3 vols. medium 8vo. price 63s. cloth.

Chemistry, Medicine, Surgery, and the Allied Sciences.

A DICTIONARY of CHEMISTRY and the Allied Branches of other Sciences. By HENRY WATTS, F.R.S. assisted by eminent Contributors. Complete in 5 vols. medium 8vo. £7 3s.

ELEMENTS of CHEMISTRY, Theoretical and Practical. By W. ALLEN MILLER, M.D. late Prof. of Chemistry, King's Coll. London. Fourth Edition. 3 vols. 8vo. £3. PART I. CHEMICAL PHYSICS, 15s. PART II. INORGANIC CHEMISTRY, 21s. PART III. ORGANIC CHEMISTRY, 24s.

A MANUAL of CHEMISTRY, Descriptive and Theoretical. By WILLIAM ODLING, M.B. F.R.S. PART I. 8vo. 9s. PART II. just ready.

OUTLINES of CHEMISTRY; or, Brief Notes of Chemical Facts. By WILLIAM ODLING, M.B. F.R.S. Crown 8vo. 7s. 6d.

A Course of Practical Chemistry, for the use of Medical Students. By the same Author. New Edition, with 70 Woodcuts. Crown 8vo. 7s. 6d.

Lectures on Animal Chemistry, delivered at the Royal College of Physicians in 1865. By the same Author. Crown 8vo. 4s. 6d.

Lectures on the Chemical Changes of Carbon. Delivered at the Royal Institution of Great Britain. By the same Author. Crown 8vo. price 4s. 6d.

SELECT METHODS in CHEMICAL ANALYSIS, chiefly INORGANIC. By WILLIAM CROOKES, F.R.S. With 22 Woodcuts. Crown 8vo. price 12s. 6d.

A TREATISE on MEDICAL ELECTRICITY, THEORETICAL and PRACTICAL; and its Use in the Treatment of Paralysis, Neuralgia, and other Diseases. By JULIUS ALTHAUS, M.D. &c. Second Edition, revised and partly re-written. Post 8vo. with Plate and 2 Woodcuts, price 15s.

The DIAGNOSIS, PATHOLOGY, and TREATMENT of DISEASES of Women: including the Diagnosis of Pregnancy. By GRAILY HEWITT, M.D. Second Edition, enlarged; with 116 Woodcut Illustrations. 8vo. 24s.

On SOME DISORDERS of the NERVOUS SYSTEM in CHILDHOOD; being the Lumleian Lectures delivered before the Royal College of Physicians in March 1871. By CHARLES WEST, M.D. Crown 8vo. price 5s.

LECTURES on the DISEASES of INFANCY and CHILDHOOD. By CHARLES WEST, M.D. &c. Fifth Edition, revised and enlarged. 8vo. 16s.

A SYSTEM of SURGERY, Theoretical and Practical. In Treatises by Various Authors. Edited by T. HOLMES, M.A. &c. Surgeon and Lecturer on Surgery at St. George's Hospital, and Surgeon-in-Chief to the Metropolitan Police. Second Edition, thoroughly revised, with numerous Illustrations. 5 vols. 8vo. £5 5s.

The SURGICAL TREATMENT of CHILDREN'S DISEASES. By T. HOLMES, M.A. &c. late Surgeon to the Hospital for Sick Children. Second Edition, with 9 Plates and 112 Woodcuts. 8vo. 21s.

LECTURES on the PRINCIPLES and PRACTICE of PHYSIC. By Sir THOMAS WATSON, Bart. M.D. Fifth Edition, thoroughly revised. 2 vols. 8vo. price 36s.

LECTURES on SURGICAL PATHOLOGY. By Sir JAMES PAGET, Bart. F.R.S. Third Edition, revised and re-edited by the Author and Professor W. TURNER, M.B. 8vo. with 131 Woodcuts, 21s.

COOPER'S DICTIONARY of PRACTICAL SURGERY and Encyclopædia of Surgical Science. New Edition, brought down to the present time. By S. A. LANE, Surgeon to St. Mary's Hospital, assisted by various Eminent Surgeons. VOL. II. 8vo. completing the work.   [In the press.

On CHRONIC BRONCHITIS, especially as connected with GOUT, EMPHYSEMA, and DISEASES of the HEART. By E. HEADLAM GREENHOW, M.D. F.R.C.P. &c. 8vo. 7s. 6d.

The CLIMATE of the SOUTH of FRANCE as SUITED to INVALIDS; with Notices of Mediterranean and other Winter Stations. By C. T. WILLIAMS, M.A. M.D. Oxon. Assistant-Physician to the Hospital for Consumption at Brompton. Second Edition. Crown 8vo. 6s.

REPORTS on the PROGRESS of PRACTICAL and SCIENTIFIC MEDICINE in Different Parts of the World. Edited by HORACE DOBELL, M.D. assisted by numerous and distinguished Coadjutors. Vols. I. and II. 8vo. 18s. each.

PULMONARY CONSUMPTION: its Nature, Varieties, and Treatment: with an Analysis of One Thousand Cases to exemplify its Duration. By C. J. B. WILLIAMS, M.D. F.R.S. and C. T. WILLIAMS, M.A. M.D. Oxon. Post 8vo. price 10s. 6d.

CLINICAL LECTURES on DISEASES of the LIVER, JAUNDICE, and ABDOMINAL DROPSY. By CHARLES MURCHISON, M.D. Post 8vo. with 25 Woodcuts, 10s. 6d.

ANATOMY, DESCRIPTIVE and SURGICAL. By HENRY GRAY, F.R.S. With about 400 Woodcuts from Dissections. Fifth Edition, by T. HOLMES, M.A. Cantab. with a new Introduction by the Editor. Royal 8vo. 28s.

CLINICAL NOTES on DISEASES of the LARYNX, investigated and treated with the assistance of the Laryngoscope. By W. MARCET, M.D. F.R.S. Crown 8vo. with 5 Lithographs, 6s.

OUTLINES of PHYSIOLOGY, Human and Comparative. By JOHN MARSHALL, F.R.C.S. Surgeon to the University College Hospital. 2 vols. crown 8vo. with 122 Woodcuts, 32s.

PHYSIOLOGICAL ANATOMY and PHYSIOLOGY of MAN. By the late R. B. TODD, M.D. F.R.S. and W. BOWMAN, F.R.S. of King's College. With numerous Illustrations. VOL. II. 8vo. 25s.
VOL. I. New Edition by Dr. LIONEL S. BEALE, F.R.S. in course of publication, with many Illustrations. PARTS I. and II. price 7s. 6d. each.

COPLAND'S DICTIONARY of PRACTICAL MEDICINE, abridged from the larger work and throughout brought down to the present State of Medical Science. 8vo. 36s.

REIMANN'S HANDBOOK of ANILINE and its DERIVATIVES; a Treatise on the Manufacture of Aniline and Aniline Colours. Edited by WILLIAM CROOKES, F.R.S. With 5 Woodcuts. 8vo. 10s. 6d.

On the MANUFACTURE of BEET-ROOT SUGAR in ENGLAND and IRELAND. By WILLIAM CROOKES, F.R.S. Crown 8vo. with 11 Woodcuts, 8s. 6d.

A MANUAL of MATERIA MEDICA and THERAPEUTICS, abridged from Dr. PEREIRA'S *Elements* by F. J. FARRE, M.D. assisted by R. BENTLEY, M.R.C.S. and by R. WARINGTON, F.R.S. 8vo. with 90 Woodcuts, 21s.

THOMSON'S CONSPECTUS of the BRITISH PHARMACOPŒIA. 25th Edition, corrected by E. LLOYD BIRKETT, M.D. 18mo. price 6s.

The Fine Arts, and Illustrated Editions.

IN FAIRYLAND; Pictures from the Elf-World. By RICHARD DOYLE. With a Poem by W. ALLINGHAM. With Sixteen Plates, containing Thirty-six Designs printed in Colours. Folio, 31s. 6d.

LIFE of JOHN GIBSON, R.A. SCULPTOR.   Edited by Lady EASTLAKE. 8vo. 10s. 6d.

MATERIALS for a HISTORY of OIL PAINTING. By Sir CHARLES LOCKE EASTLAKE, sometime President of the Royal Academy. 2 vols. 8vo. price 30s.

HALF-HOUR LECTURES on the HISTORY and PRACTICE of the Fine and Ornamental Arts. By WILLIAM B. SCOTT. New Edition, revised by the Author; with 50 Woodcuts. Crown 8vo. 8s. 6d.

ALBERT DURER, HIS LIFE and WORKS; including Auto-biographical Papers and Complete Catalogues. By WILLIAM B. SCOTT. With Six Etchings by the Author, and other Illustrations. 8vo. 16s.

SIX LECTURES on HARMONY, delivered at the Royal Institution of Great Britain in the Year 1867. By G. A. MACFARREN. With nume-rous engraved Musical Examples and Specimens. 8vo. 10s. 6d.

The CHORALE BOOK for ENGLAND: the Hymns translated by Miss C. WINKWORTH; the Tunes arranged by Prof. W. S. BENNETT and OTTO GOLDSCHMIDT. Fcp. 4to. 12s. 6d.

The NEW TESTAMENT, illustrated with Wood Engravings after the Early Masters, chiefly of the Italian School. Crown 4to. 63s. cloth, gilt top; or £5 5s. elegantly bound in morocco.

LYRA GERMANICA; the Christian Year. Translated by CATHERINE WINKWORTH; with 125 Illustrations on Wood drawn by J. LEIGHTON. F.S.A. 4to. 21s.

LYRA GERMANICA; the Christian Life. Translated by CATHERINE WINKWORTH; with about 200 Woodcut Illustrations by J. LEIGHTON, F.S.A. and other Artists. 4to. 21s.

The LIFE of MAN SYMBOLISED by the MONTHS of the YEAR. Text selected by R. PIGOT; Illustrations on Wood from Original Designs by J. LEIGHTON, F.S.A. 4to. 42s.

CATS' and FARLIE'S MORAL EMBLEMS; with Aphorisms, Adages, and Proverbs of all Nations. 121 Illustrations on Wood by J. LEIGHTON, F.S.A. Text selected by R. PIGOT. Imperial 8vo. 31s. 6d.

SACRED and LEGENDARY ART. By Mrs. JAMESON.

Legends of the Saints and Martyrs. Fifth Edition, with 19 Etchings and 187 Woodcuts. 2 vols. square crown 8vo. 31s. 6d.

Legends of the Monastic Orders. Third Edition, with 11 Etchings and 88 Woodcuts. 1 vol. square crown 8vo. 21s.

Legends of the Madonna. Third Edition, with 27 Etchings and 165 Woodcuts. 1 vol. square crown 8vo. 21s.

The History of Our Lord, with that of his Types and Precursors. Completed by Lady EASTLAKE. Revised Edition, with 31 Etchings and 281 Woodcuts. 2 vols. square crown 8vo. 42s.

The Useful Arts, Manufactures, &c.

HISTORY of the GOTHIC REVIVAL; an Attempt to shew how far the taste for Mediæval Architecture was retained in England during the last two centuries, and has been re-developed in the present. By CHARLES L. EASTLAKE, Architect. With many Illustrations. Imp. 8vo. price 31s. 6d.

GWILT'S ENCYCLOPÆDIA of ARCHITECTURE, with above 1,600 Engravings on Wood. Fifth Edition, revised and enlarged by WYATT PAPWORTH. 8vo. 52s. 6d.

A MANUAL of ARCHITECTURE: being a Concise History and Explanation of the principal Styles of European Architecture, Ancient, Mediæval, and Renaissance; with a Glossary of Technical Terms. By THOMAS MITCHELL. Crown 8vo. with 150 Woodcuts, 10s. 6d.

ITALIAN SCULPTORS: being a History of Sculpture in Northern, Southern, and Eastern Italy. By C. C. PERKINS. With 30 Etchings and 13 Wood Engravings. Imperial 8vo. 42s.

TUSCAN SCULPTORS, their Lives, Works, and Times. With 45 Etchings and 28 Woodcuts from Original Drawings and Photographs. By the same Author. 2 vols. imperial 8vo. 63s.

HINTS on HOUSEHOLD TASTE in FURNITURE, UPHOLSTERY, and other Details. By CHARLES L. EASTLAKE, Architect. Second Edition, with about 90 Illustrations. Square crown 8vo. 18s.

The ENGINEER'S HANDBOOK; explaining the Principles which should guide the Young Engineer in the Construction of Machinery. By C. S. LOWNDES. Post 8vo. 5s.

PRINCIPLES of MECHANISM, designed for the Use of Students in the Universities, and for Engineering Students generally. By R. WILLIS, M.A. F.R.S. &c. Jacksonian Professor in the University of Cambridge. Second Edition, enlarged; with 374 Woodcuts. 8vo. 18s.

LATHES and TURNING, Simple, Mechanical, and ORNAMENTAL. By W. HENRY NORTHCOTT. With about 240 Illustrations on Steel and Wood. 8vo. 18s.

URE'S DICTIONARY of ARTS, MANUFACTURES, and MINES. Sixth Edition, chiefly rewritten and greatly enlarged by ROBERT HUNT, F.R.S. assisted by numerous Contributors eminent in Science and the Arts, and familiar with Manufactures. With above 2,000 Woodcuts. 3 vols. medium 8vo. price £4 14s. 6d.

D

HANDBOOK of **PRACTICAL TELEGRAPHY**. By R. S. CULLEY, Memb. Inst. C.E. Engineer-in-Chief of Telegraphs to the Post Office. Fifth Edition, with 118 Woodcuts and 9 Plates. 8vo. price 14s.

ENCYCLOPÆDIA of **CIVIL ENGINEERING**, Historical, Theoretical, and Practical. By E. CRESY, C.E. With above 3,000 Woodcuts. 8vo. 42s.

TREATISE on **MILLS** and **MILLWORK**. By Sir W. FAIRBAIRN, Bart. F.R.S. New Edition, with 18 Plates and 822 Woodcuts. 2 vols. 8vo. 32s.

USEFUL INFORMATION for **ENGINEERS**. By the same Author. FIRST, SECOND, and THIRD SERIES, with many Plates and Woodcuts, 3 vols. crown 8vo. 10s. 6d. each.

The APPLICATION of **CAST** and **WROUGHT IRON** to Building Purposes. By Sir W. FAIRBAIRN, Bart. F.R.S. Fourth Edition, enlarged; with 6 Plates and 118 Woodcuts. 8vo. price 16s.

IRON SHIP BUILDING, its History and Progress, as comprised in a Series of Experimental Researches. By the same Author. With 4 Plates and 180 Woodcuts. 8vo. 18s.

A TREATISE on the **STEAM ENGINE**, in its various Applications to Mines, Mills, Steam Navigation, Railways and Agriculture. By J. BOURNE, C.E. Eighth Edition; with Portrait, 37 Plates, and 546 Woodcuts. 4to. 42s.

CATECHISM of the **STEAM ENGINE**, in its various Applications to Mines, Mills, Steam Navigation, Railways, and Agriculture. By the same Author. With 89 Woodcuts. Fcp. 6s.

HANDBOOK of the **STEAM ENGINE**. By the same Author, forming a KEY to the Catechism of the Steam Engine, with 67 Woodcuts. Fcp. 9s.

BOURNE'S RECENT IMPROVEMENTS in the **STEAM ENGINE** in its various applications to Mines, Mills, Steam Navigation, Railways, and Agriculture. Being a Supplement to the Author's 'Catechism of the Steam Engine.' By JOHN BOURNE, C.E. New Edition, including many New Examples; with 124 Woodcuts. Fcp. 8vo. 6s.

A TREATISE on the **SCREW PROPELLER, SCREW VESSELS**, and Screw Engines, as adapted for purposes of Peace and War; with Notices of other Methods of Propulsion, Tables of the Dimensions and Performance of Screw Steamers, and detailed Specifications of Ships and Engines. By J. BOURNE, C.E. New Edition, with 54 Plates and 287 Woodcuts. 4to. 63s.

EXAMPLES of **MODERN STEAM, AIR, and GAS ENGINES** of the most Approved Types, as employed for Pumping, for Driving Machinery, for Locomotion, and for Agriculture, minutely and practically described. By JOHN BOURNE, C.E. In course of publication in 24 Parts, price 2s. 6d. each, forming One volume 4to. with about 50 Plates and 400 Woodcuts.

A HISTORY of the **MACHINE-WROUGHT HOSIERY** and **LACE** Manufactures. By WILLIAM FELKIN, F.L.S. F.S.S. Royal 8vo. 21s.

PRACTICAL TREATISE on **METALLURGY**, adapted from the last German Edition of Professor KERL's *Metallurgy* by W. CROOKES, F.R.S. &c. and E. RÖHRIG, Ph.D. M.E. With 625 Woodcuts. 3 vols. 8vo. price £4 19s.

MITCHELL'S MANUAL of **PRACTICAL ASSAYING**. Third Edition, for the most part re-written, with all the recent Discoveries incorporated, by W. CROOKES, F.R.S. With 188 Woodcuts. 8vo. 28s.

The ART of PERFUMERY; the History and Theory of Odours, and the Methods of Extracting the Aromas of Plants. By Dr. PIESSE, F.C.S. Third Edition, with 53 Woodcuts. Crown 8vo. 10s. 6d.

Chemical, Natural, and Physical Magic, for Juveniles during the Holidays. By the same Author. Third Edition, with 38 Woodcuts. Fcp. 6s.

LOUDON'S ENCYCLOPÆDIA of AGRICULTURE: comprising the Laying-out, Improvement, and Management of Landed Property, and the Cultivation and Economy of the Productions of Agriculture. With 1,100 Woodcuts. 8vo. 21s.

Loudon's Encyclopædia of Gardening: comprising the Theory and Practice of Horticulture, Floriculture, Arboriculture, and Landscape Gardening. With 1,000 Woodcuts. 8vo. 21s.

BAYLDON'S ART of VALUING RENTS and TILLAGES, and Claims of Tenants upon Quitting Farms, both at Michaelmas and Lady-Day. Eighth Edition, revised by J. C. MORTON. 8vo. 10s. 6d.

Religious and Moral Works.

OLD TESTAMENT SYNONYMS, their BEARING on CHRISTIAN FAITH and PRACTICE. By the Rev. R. B. GIRDLESTONE. M.A. 8vo. [Nearly ready.

An INTRODUCTION to the THEOLOGY of the CHURCH of ENGLAND, in an Exposition of the Thirty-nine Articles. By the Rev. T. P. BOULTBEE, M.A. Fcp. 8vo. price 6s.

FUNDAMENTALS; or, Bases of Belief concerning MAN and GOD: a Handbook of Mental, Moral, and Religious Philosophy. By the Rev. T. GRIFFITH, M.A. 8vo. price 6s. 6d.

PRAYERS SELECTED from the COLLECTION of the late BARON BUNSEN, and Translated by CATHERINE WINKWORTH. PART I. For the Family. PART II. Prayers and Meditations for Private Use. Fcp. 8vo. price 3s. 6d.

The STUDENT'S COMPENDIUM of the BOOK of COMMON PRAYER; being Notes Historical and Explanatory of the Liturgy of the Church of England. By the Rev. H. ALLDEN NASH. Fcp. 8vo. price 2s. 6d.

The BIBLE and POPULAR THEOLOGY; a Re-statement of Truths and Principles, with special reference to recent works of Dr. Liddon, Lord Hatherley, and the Right Hon. W. E. Gladstone. By G. VANCE SMITH, B.A. Ph.D. 8vo. price 7s. 6d.

The TRUTH of the BIBLE: Evidence from the Mosaic and other Records of Creation; the Origin and Antiquity of Man; the Science of Scripture; and from the Archæology of Different Nations of the Earth. By the Rev. B. W. SAVILE, M.A. Crown 8vo. price 7s. 6d.

CHURCHES and their CREEDS. By the Rev. Sir PHILIP PERRING, Bart. late Scholar of Trin. Coll. Cambridge, and University Medallist. Crown 8vo. price 10s. 6d.

CONSIDERATIONS on the REVISION of the ENGLISH NEW TESTAMENT. By C. J. ELLICOTT, D.D. Lord Bishop of Gloucester and Bristol. Post 8vo. price 5s. 6d.

An EXPOSITION of the 39 ARTICLES, Historical and Doctrinal. By E. HAROLD BROWNE, D.D. Lord Bishop of Ely. Ninth Edit. 8vo. 14s.

The LIFE and EPISTLES of ST. PAUL. By the Rev. W. J. CONYBEARE, M.A., and the Very Rev. J. S. HOWSON, D.D. Dean of Chester:—
LIBRARY EDITION, with all the Original Illustrations, Maps, Landscapes on Steel, Woodcuts, &c. 2 vols. 4to. 48s.

INTERMEDIATE EDITION, with a Selection of Maps, Plates, and Woodcuts. 2 vols. square crown 8vo. 31s. 6d.

STUDENT'S EDITION, revised and condensed, with 46 Illustrations and Maps. 1 vol. crown 8vo. price 9s.

The VOYAGE and SHIPWRECK of ST. PAUL; with Dissertations on the Life and Writings of St. Luke and the Ships and Navigation of the Ancients. By JAMES SMITH, F.R.S. Third Edition. Crown 8vo. 10s. 6d.

A CRITICAL and GRAMMATICAL COMMENTARY on ST. PAUL'S Epistles. By C. J. ELLICOTT, D.D. Lord Bishop of Gloucester & Bristol. 8vo.

Galatians, Fourth Edition, 8s. 6d.

Ephesians, Fourth Edition, 8s. 6d.

Pastoral Epistles, Fourth Edition, 10s. 6d.

Philippians, Colossians, and Philemon, Third Edition, 10s. 6d.

Thessalonians, Third Edition, 7s. 6d.

HISTORICAL LECTURES on the LIFE of OUR LORD JESUS CHRIST: being the Hulsean Lectures for 1859. By C. J. ELLICOTT, D.D. Lord Bishop of Gloucester and Bristol. Fifth Edition. 8vo. price 12s.

EVIDENCE of the TRUTH of the CHRISTIAN RELIGION derived from the Literal Fulfilment of Prophecy. By ALEXANDER KEITH, D.D. 37th Edition, with numerous Plates, in square 8vo. 12s. 6d.; also the 39th Edition, in post 8vo. with 5 Plates, 6s.

History and Destiny of the World and Church, according to Scripture. By the same Author. Square 8vo. with 40 Illustrations, 10s.

An INTRODUCTION to the STUDY of the NEW TESTAMENT, Critical, Exegetical, and Theological. By the Rev. S. DAVIDSON, D.D. LL.D. 2 vols. 8vo. 30s.

HARTWELL HORNE'S INTRODUCTION to the CRITICAL STUDY and Knowledge of the Holy Scriptures, as last revised; with 4 Maps and 22 Woodcuts and Facsimiles. 4 vols. 8vo. 42s.

Horne's Compendious Introduction to the Study of the Bible. Re-edited by the Rev. JOHN AYRE, M.A. With Maps, &c. Post 8vo. 6s.

EWALD'S HISTORY of ISRAEL to the DEATH of MOSES. Translated from the German. Edited, with a Preface and an Appendix, by RUSSELL MARTINEAU, M.A. Second Edition. 2 vols. 8vo. 24s.

The HISTORY and LITERATURE of the ISRAELITES, according to the Old Testament and the Apocrypha. By C. DE ROTHSCHILD and A. DE ROTHSCHILD. Second Edition, revised. 2 vols. post 8vo. with Two Maps, price 12s. 6d.

The SEE of ROME in the MIDDLE AGES. By the Rev. OSWALD J. REICHEL, B.C.L. and M.A. 8vo. price 18s.

The TREASURY of BIBLE KNOWLEDGE; being a Dictionary of the Books, Persons, Places, Events, and other matters of which mention is made in Holy Scripture. By Rev. J. AYRE, M.A. With Maps, 16 Plates, and numerous Woodcuts. Fcp. 8vo. price 6s. cloth, or 9s. 6d. neatly bound in calf.

The GREEK TESTAMENT; with Notes, Grammatical and Exegetical. By the Rev. W. WEBSTER, M.A. and the Rev. W. F. WILKINSON, M.A. 2 vols. 8vo. £2 4s.

EVERY-DAY SCRIPTURE DIFFICULTIES explained and illustrated. By J. E. PRESCOTT, M.A. VOL. I. *Matthew* and *Mark*; VOL. II. *Luke* and *John*. 2 vols. 8vo. 9s. each.

The PENTATEUCH and BOOK of JOSHUA CRITICALLY EXAMINED. By the Right Rev. J. W. COLENSO, D.D. Lord Bishop of Natal. People's Edition, in 1 vol. crown 8vo. 6s.

SIX SERMONS on the FOUR CARDINAL VIRTUES in relation to the Public and Private Life of Catholics. By the Rev. ORBY SHIPLEY, M.A. Crown 8vo. with Frontispiece, price 7s. 6d.

The FORMATION of CHRISTENDOM. By T. W. ALLIES. Parts I. and II. 8vo. price 12s. each Part.

ENGLAND and CHRISTENDOM. By ARCHBISHOP MANNING, D.D. Post 8vo. price 10s. 6d.

CHRISTENDOM'S DIVISIONS, PART I., a Philosophical Sketch of the Divisions of the Christian Family in East and West. By EDMUND S. FFOULKES. Post 8vo. price 7s. 6d.

Christendom's Divisions, PART II. Greeks and Latins, being a History of their Dissensions and Overtures for Peace down to the Reformation. By the same Author. Post 8vo. 15s.

A VIEW of the SCRIPTURE REVELATIONS CONCERNING a FUTURE STATE. By RICHARD WHATELY, D.D. late Archbishop of Dublin. Ninth Edition. Fcp. 8vo. 5s.

THOUGHTS for the AGE. By ELIZABETH M. SEWELL, Author of 'Amy Herbert' &c. New Edition, revised. Fcp. 8vo. price 5s.

Passing Thoughts on Religion. By the same Author. Fcp. 8vo. 5s.

Self-Examination before Confirmation. By the same Author. 32mo. price 1s. 6d.

Readings for a Month Preparatory to Confirmation, from Writers of the Early and English Church. By the same Author. Fcp. 4s.

Readings for Every Day in Lent, compiled from the Writings of Bishop JEREMY TAYLOR. By the same Author. Fcp. 5s.

Preparation for the Holy Communion; the Devotions chiefly from the works of JEREMY TAYLOR. By the same Author. 32mo. 3s.

THOUGHTS for the HOLY WEEK for Young Persons. By the Author of 'Amy Herbert.' New Edition. Fcp. 8vo. 2s.

PRINCIPLES of EDUCATION Drawn from Nature and Revelation, and applied to Female Education in the Upper Classes. By the Author of 'Amy Herbert.' 2 vols. fcp. 12s. 6d.

SINGERS and SONGS of the CHURCH: being Biographical Sketches of the Hymn-Writers in all the principal Collections; with Notes on their Psalms and Hymns. By JOSIAH MILLER, M.A. Post 8vo. price 10s. 6d.

LYRA GERMANICA, translated from the German by Miss C. WINKWORTH. FIRST SERIES, Hymns for the Sundays and Chief Festivals. SECOND SERIES, the Christian Life. Fcp. 3s. 6d. each SERIES.

'SPIRITUAL SONGS' for the SUNDAYS and HOLIDAYS throughout the Year. By J. S. B. MONSELL, LL.D. Vicar of Egham and Rural Dean. Fourth Edition, Sixth Thousand. Fcp. 4s. 6d.

The BEATITUDES: Abasement before God ; Sorrow for Sin ; Meekness of Spirit; Desire for Holiness; Gentleness; Purity of Heart; the Peacemakers; Sufferings for Christ. By the same. Third Edition. Fcp. 3s. 6d.

His PRESENCE—not his MEMORY, 1855. By the same Author, in Memory of his Son. Sixth Edition. 16mo. 1s.

LYRA EUCHARISTICA; Hymns and Verses on the Holy Communion, Ancient and Modern: with other Poems. Edited by the Rev. ORBY SHIPLEY, M.A. Second Edition. Fcp. 5s.

Lyra Messianica; Hymns and Verses on the Life of Christ, Ancient and Modern; with other Poems. By the same Editor. Second Edition, altered and enlarged. Fcp. 5s.

Lyra Mystica; Hymns and Verses on Sacred Subjects, Ancient and Modern. By the same Editor. Fcp. 5s.

ENDEAVOURS after the CHRISTIAN LIFE: Discourses. By JAMES MARTINEAU. Fourth Edition, carefully revised. Post 8vo. 7s. 6d.

INVOCATION of SAINTS and ANGELS, for the use of Members of the English Church. Edited by the Rev. ORBY SHIPLEY. 24mo. 3s. 6d.

WHATELY'S INTRODUCTORY LESSONS on the CHRISTIAN Evidences. 18mo. 6d.

FOUR DISCOURSES of CHRYSOSTOM, chiefly on the Parable of the Rich Man and Lazarus. Translated by F. ALLEN, B.A. Crown 8vo. 3s. 6d.

BISHOP JEREMY TAYLOR'S ENTIRE WORKS. With Life by BISHOP HEBER. Revised and corrected by the Rev. C. P. EDEN, 10 vols. price £5 5s.

Travels, Voyages, &c.

HOW to SEE NORWAY. By Captain J. R. CAMPBELL. With Map and 5 Woodcuts. Fcp. 8vo. price 5s.

PAU and the PYRENEES. By Count HENRY RUSSELL, [Member of the Alpine Club, &c. With 2 Maps. Fcp. 8vo. price 5s.

SCENES in the SUNNY SOUTH; including the Atlas Mountains and the Oases of the Sahara in Algeria. By Lieut.-Col. the Hon. C. S. VEREKER, M.A. Commandant of the Limerick Artillery Militia. 2 vols. post 8vo. price 21s.

The PLAYGROUND of EUROPE. By LESLIE STEPHEN, late President of the Alpine Club. With 4 Illustrations engraved on Wood by E. Whymper. Crown 8vo. price 10s. 6d.

CADORE; or, TITIAN'S COUNTRY. By JOSIAH GILBERT, one of the Authors of 'The Dolomite Mountains.' With Map, Facsimile, and 40 Illustrations. Imperial 8vo. 31s. 6d.

HOURS of EXERCISE in the ALPS. By JOHN TYNDALL, LL.D. F.R.S. Second Edition, with 7 Woodcuts by E. WHYMPER. Crown 8vo. price 12s. 6d.

TRAVELS in the **CENTRAL CAUCASUS** and **BASHAN.** Including Visits to Ararat and Tabreez and Ascents of Kazbek and Elbruz. By D. W. FRESHFIELD. Square crown 8vo. with Maps, &c. 18s.

PICTURES in **TYROL** and **Elsewhere.** From a Family Sketch-Book. By the Authoress of 'A Voyage en Zigzag,' &c. Second Edition. Small 4to. with numerous Illustrations, 21s.

HOW WE SPENT the **SUMMER**; or, a Voyage en Zigzag in Switzerland and Tyrol with some Members of the ALPINE CLUB. From the Sketch-Book of one of the Party. In oblong 4to. with 300 Illustrations, 15s.

BEATEN TRACKS; or, Pen and Pencil Sketches in Italy. By the Authoress of 'A Voyage en Zigzag.' With 42 Plates, containing about 200 Sketches from Drawings made on the Spot. 8vo. 16s.

MAP of the **CHAIN** of **MONT BLANC**, from an actual Survey in 1863—1864. By A. ADAMS-REILLY, F.R.G.S. M.A.C. Published under the Authority of the Alpine Club. In Chromolithography on extra stout drawing-paper 28in. × 17in. price 10s. or mounted on canvas in a folding case, 12s. 6d.

WESTWARD by RAIL; the New Route to the East. By W. F. RAE. With Map shewing the Lines of Rail between the Atlantic and the Pacific and Sections of the Railway. Second Edition, enlarged. Post 8vo. 10s. 6d.

HISTORY of DISCOVERY in our AUSTRALASIAN COLONIES, Australia, Tasmania, and New Zealand, from the Earliest Date to the Present Day. By WILLIAM HOWITT. 2 vols. 8vo. with 3 Maps, 20s.

The CAPITAL of the TYCOON; a Narrative of a Three Years' Residence in Japan. By Sir RUTHERFORD ALCOCK, K.C.B. 2 vols. 8vo. with numerous Illustrations, 42s.

ZIGZAGGING AMONGST DOLOMITES. By the Author of 'How we Spent the Summer, or a Voyage en Zigzag in Switzerland and Tyrol.' With upwards of 300 Illustrations by the Author. Oblong 4to. price 15s.

The DOLOMITE MOUNTAINS; Excursions through Tyrol, Carinthia, Carniola, and Friuli, 1861-1863. By J. GILBERT and G. C. CHURCHILL, F.R.G.S. With numerous Illustrations. Square crown 8vo. 21s.

GUIDE to the PYRENEES, for the use of Mountaineers. By CHARLES PACKE. 2nd Edition, with Map and Illustrations. Cr. 8vo. 7s. 6d.

The ALPINE GUIDE. By JOHN BALL, M.R.I.A. late President of the Alpine Club. Thoroughly Revised Editions, in Three Volumes, post 8vo. with Maps and other Illustrations:—

GUIDE to the WESTERN ALPS, including Mont Blanc, Monte Rosa, Zermatt, &c. Price 6s. 6d.

GUIDE to the CENTRAL ALPS, including all the Oberland District. Price 7s. 6d.

GUIDE to the EASTERN ALPS, price 10s. 6d.

Introduction on Alpine Travelling in General, and on the Geology of the Alps, price 1s. Each of the Three Volumes or Parts of the *Alpine Guide* may be had with this INTRODUCTION prefixed, price 1s. extra.

The NORTHERN HEIGHTS of LONDON; or, Historical Associations of Hampstead, Highgate, Muswell Hill, Hornsey, and Islington. By WILLIAM HOWITT. With about 40 Woodcuts. Square crown 8vo. 21s.

VISITS to REMARKABLE PLACES: Old Halls, Battle-Fields, and Stones Illustrative of Striking Passages in English History and Poetry. By WILLIAM HOWITT. 2 vols. square crown 8vo. with Woodcuts, 25s.

The RURAL LIFE of ENGLAND. By the same Author. With Woodcuts by Bewick and Williams. Medium 8vo. 12s. 6d.

PILGRIMAGES in the PYRENEES and LANDES. By DENYS SHYNE LAWLOR. Crown 8vo. with Frontispiece and Vignette, price 15s.

Works of *Fiction.*

NOVELS and TALES. By the Right Hon. B. DISRAELI, M.P. Cabinet Edition, complete in Ten Volumes, crown 8vo. price 6s. each, as follows:—

LOTHAIR. 6s.	HENRIETTA TEMPLE, 6s.
CONINGSBY, 6s.	CONTARINI FLEMING, &c. 6s.
SYBIL, 6s.	ALROY, IXION, &c. 6s.
TANCRED, 6s.	*The* YOUNG DUKE, &c. 6s.
VENETIA, 6s.	VIVIAN GREY, 6s.

The MODERN NOVELIST'S LIBRARY. Each Work, in crown 8vo. complete in a Single Volume:—

MELVILLE'S GLADIATORS. 2s. boards; 2s. 6d. cloth.
———— GOOD FOR NOTHING, 2s. boards; 2s. 6d. cloth.
———— HOLMBY HOUSE, 2s. boards; 2s. 6d. cloth.
———— INTERPRETER, 2s. boards; 2s. 6d. cloth.
———— KATE COVENTRY, 2s. boards; 2s. 6d. cloth.
———— QUEEN'S MARIES, 2s. boards; 2s. 6d. cloth.
TROLLOPE'S WARDEN, 1s. 6d. boards; 2s. cloth.
———— BARCHESTER TOWERS, 2s. boards; 2s. 6d. cloth.
BRAMLEY-MOORE'S SIX SISTERS *of the* VALLEYS, 2s. boards; 2s. 6d. cloth.

IERNE; a Tale. By W. STEUART TRENCH, Author of 'Realities of Irish Life.' Second Edition. 2 vols. post 8vo. price 21s.

The HOME at HEATHERBRAE; a Tale. By the Author of 'Everley.' Fcp. 8vo. price 6s.

CABINET EDITION of STORIES and TALES by MISS SEWELL:—

AMY HERBERT, 2s. 6d.	IVORS, 3s. 6d.
GERTRUDE, 2s. 6d.	KATHARINE ASHTON, 3s. 6d.
The EARL'S DAUGHTER, 2s. 6d.	MARGARET PERCIVAL, 5s.
EXPERIENCE *of* LIFE, 2s. 6d.	LANETON PARSONAGE, 4s. 6d.
CLEVE HALL, 3s. 6d.	URSULA, 4s. 6d.

STORIES and TALES. By E. M. SEWELL. Comprising:—Amy Herbert; Gertrude; The Earl's Daughter; The Experience of Life; Cleve Hall; Ivors; Katharine Ashton; Margaret Percival; Laneton Parsonage; *and* Ursula. The Ten Works, complete in Eight Volumes, crown 8vo. bound in leather, and contained in a Box, price 42s.

A Glimpse of the World. By the Author of 'Amy Herbert.' Fcp. 7s. 6d.

The Journal of a Home Life. By the same Author. Post 8vo. 9s. 6d.

After Life; a Sequel to 'The Journal of a Home Life.' Price 10s. 6d.

UNCLE PETER'S FAIRY TALE for the NINETEENTH CENTURY. Edited by E. M. SEWELL, Author of 'Amy Herbert,' &c. Fcp. 8vo. 7s. 6d.

THE GIANT; A Witch's Story for English Boys. By the same Author and Editor. Fcp. 8vo. price 6s.

WONDERFUL STORIES from NORWAY, SWEDEN, and ICELAND. Adapted and arranged by JULIA GODDARD. With an Introductory Essay by the Rev. G. W. Cox, M.A. and Six Woodcuts. Square post 8vo. 6s.

A VISIT to MY DISCONTENTED COUSIN. Reprinted, with some Additions, from Fraser's Magazine. Crown 8vo. price 7s. 6d.

BECKER'S GALLUS; or, Roman Scenes of the Time of Augustus: with Notes and Excursuses. New Edition. Post 8vo. 7s. 6d.

BECKER'S CHARICLES; a Tale illustrative of Private Life among the Ancient Greeks: with Notes and Excursuses. New Edition. Post 8vo. 7s. 6d.

CABINET EDITION of NOVELS and TALES by G. J. WHYTE MELVILLE:—

The GLADIATORS, 5s.	HOLMBY HOUSE, 5s.
DIGBY GRAND, 5s.	GOOD for NOTHING, 6s.
KATE COVENTRY, 5s.	The QUEEN'S MARIES, 6s.
GENERAL BOUNCE, 5s.	The INTERPRETER, 5s.

TALES of ANCIENT GREECE. By GEORGE W. COX, M.A. late Scholar of Trin. Coll. Oxon. Crown 8vo. price 6s. 6d.

A MANUAL of MYTHOLOGY, in the form of Question and Answer. By the same Author. Fcp. 3s.

OUR CHILDREN'S STORY, by one of their Gossips. By the Author of ' Voyage en Zigzag,' ' Pictures in Tyrol,' &c. Small 4to. with Sixty Illustrations by the Author, price 10s. 6d.

Poetry and The Drama.

THOMAS MOORE'S POETICAL WORKS, the only Editions containing the Author's last Copyright Additions:—
CABINET EDITION, 10 vols. fcp. 8vo. price 35s.
SHAMROCK EDITION, crown 8vo. price 3s. 6d.
RUBY EDITION, crown 8vo. with Portrait, price 6s.
LIBRARY EDITION, medium 8vo. Portrait and Vignette, 14s.
PEOPLE'S EDITION. square crown 8vo. with Portrait, &c. 10s. 6d.

MOORE'S IRISH MELODIES, Maclise's Edition, with 161 Steel Plates from Original Drawings. Super-royal 8vo. 31s. 6d.

Miniature Edition of Moore's Irish Melodies with Maclise's Designs (as above) reduced in Lithography. Imp. 16mo. 10s. 6d.

MOORE'S LALLA ROOKH. Tenniel's Edition, with 68 Wood Engravings from original Drawings and other Illustrations. Fcp. 4to. 21s.

SOUTHEY'S POETICAL WORKS, with the Author's last Corrections and copyright Additions. Library Edition, in 1 vol. medium 8vo. with Portrait and Vignette, 14s.

LAYS of ANCIENT ROME; with Ivry and the Armada. By the Right Hon. LORD MACAULAY. 16mo. 4s. 6d.

Lord Macaulay's Lays of Ancient Rome. With 90 Illustrations on Wood, from the Antique, from Drawings by G. SCHARF. Fcp. 4to. 21s.

Miniature Edition of Lord Macaulay's Lays of Ancient Rome, with the Illustrations (as above) reduced in Lithography. Imp. 16mo. 10s. 6d.

GOLDSMITH'S POETICAL WORKS, with Wood Engravings from Designs by Members of the ETCHING CLUB. Imperial 16mo. 7s. 6d.

JOHN JERNINGHAM'S JOURNAL. Fcp. 8vo. price 3s. 6d.

POEMS OF BYGONE YEARS. Edited by the Author of 'Amy Herbert,' &c. Fcp. 8vo. price 5s.

POEMS. By JEAN INGELOW. Fifteenth Edition. Fcp. 8vo. 5s.

EUCHARIS ; a Poem. By F. REGINALD STATHAM (Francis Reynolds), Author of 'Alice Rushton, and other Poems' and 'Glaphyra, and other Poems.' Fcp. 8vo. price 3s. 6d.

POEMS by Jean Ingelow. With nearly 100 Illustrations by Eminent Artists, engraved on Wood by the Brothers DALZIEL. Fcp. 4to. 21s.

The MAD WAR PLANET, and other POEMS. By WILLIAM HOWITT, Author of 'Visits to Remarkable Places,' &c. Fcp. 8vo. price 5s.

MOPSA the FAIRY. By JEAN INGELOW. Pp. 256, with Eight Illustrations engraved on Wood. Fcp. 8vo. 6s.

A STORY of DOOM, and other Poems. By JEAN INGELOW. Third Edition. Fcp. 5s.

WORKS by EDWARD YARDLEY:—
>   FANTASTIC STORIES. Fcp. 3s. 6d.
>   MELUSINE and OTHER POEMS. Fcp. 5s.
>   HORACE's ODES, translated into English Verse. Crown 8vo. 6s.
>   SUPPLEMENTARY STORIES and POEMS. Fcp. 3s. 6d.

BOWDLER'S FAMILY SHAKSPEARE, cheaper Genuine Editions. Medium 8vo. large type, with 36 WOODCUTS, price 14s. Cabinet Edition, with the same ILLUSTRATIONS, 6 vols. fcp. 3s. 6d. each.

HORATII OPERA, Pocket Edition, with carefully corrected Text, Marginal References, and Introduction. Edited by the Rev. J. E. YONGE, M.A. Square 18mo. 4s. 6d.

HORATII OPERA. Library Edition, with Marginal References and English Notes. Edited by the Rev. J. E. YONGE. 8vo. 21s.

The ÆNEID of VIRGIL Translated into English Verse. By JOHN CONINGTON, M.A. New Edition. Crown 8vo. 9s.

ARUNDINES CAMI, sive Musarum Cantabrigiensium Lusus canori. Collegit atque edidit H. DRURY, M.A. Editio Sexta, curavit H. J. HODGSON, M.A. Crown 8vo. 7s. 6d.

HUNTING SONGS and MISCELLANEOUS VERSES. By R. E. EGERTON WARBURTON. Second Edition. Fcp. 8vo. 5s.

Rural Sports, &c.

ENCYCLOPÆDIA of RURAL SPORTS ; a complete Account, Histo-rical, Practical, and Descriptive, of Hunting, Shooting, Fishing, Racing, and all other Rural and Athletic Sports and Pastimes. By D. P. BLAINE. With above 600 Woodcuts (20 from Designs by JOHN LEECH). 8vo. 21s.

The DEAD SHOT, or Sportsman's Complete Guide; a Treatise on the Use of the Gun, Dog-breaking, Pigeon-shooting, &c. By MARKSMAN. Revised Edition. Fcp. 8vo. with Plates, 5s.

The FLY-FISHER'S ENTOMOLOGY. By ALFRED RONALDS. With coloured, Representations of the Natural and Artificial Insect. Sixth Edition; with 20 coloured Plates. 8vo. 14s.

A BOOK on ANGLING; a complete Treatise on the Art of Angling in every branch. By FRANCIS FRANCIS. Second Edition, with Portrait and 15 other Plates, plain and coloured. Post 8vo. 15s.

The BOOK of the ROACH. By GREVILLE FENNELL, of 'The Field.' Fcp. 8vo. price 2s. 6d.

WILCOCKS'S SEA-FISHERMAN; comprising the Chief Methods of Hook and Line Fishing in the British and other Seas, a Glance at Nets, and Remarks on Boats and Boating. Second Edition, enlarged; with 80 Woodcuts. Post 8vo. 12s. 6d.

HORSES and STABLES. By Colonel F. FITZWYGRAM, XV. the King's Hussars. With Twenty-four Plates of Illustrations, containing very numerous Figures engraved on Wood. 8vo. 15s.

The HORSE'S FOOT, and HOW to KEEP IT SOUND. By W. MILES, Esq. Ninth Edition, with Illustrations. Imperial 8vo. 12s. 6d.

A PLAIN TREATISE on HORSE-SHOEING. By the same Author. Sixth Edition. Post 8vo. with Illustrations, 2s. 6d.

STABLES and STABLE-FITTINGS. By the same. Imp. 8vo. with 13 Plates, 15s.

REMARKS on HORSES' TEETH, addressed to Purchasers. By the same. Post 8vo. 1s. 6d.

ROBBINS'S CAVALRY CATECHISM, or Instructions on Cavalry Exercise and Field Movements, Brigade Movements, Out-post Duty, Cavalry supporting Artillery, Artillery attached to Cavalry. 12mo. 5s.

BLAINE'S VETERINARY ART; a Treatise on the Anatomy, Physiology, and Curative Treatment of the Diseases of the Horse, Neat Cattle and Sheep. Seventh Edition, revised and enlarged by C. STEEL, M.R.C.V.S.L. 8vo. with Plates and Woodcuts, 18s.

The HORSE: with a Treatise on Draught. By WILLIAM YOUATT. New Edition, revised and enlarged. 8vo. with numerous Woodcuts, 12s. 6d.

The DOG. By the same Author. 8vo. with numerous Woodcuts, 6s.

The DOG in HEALTH and DISEASE. By STONEHENGE. With 70 Wood Engravings. Square crown 8vo. 10s. 6d.

The GREYHOUND. By STONEHENGE. Revised Edition, with 24 Portraits of Greyhounds. Square crown 8vo. 10s. 6d.

The OX; his Diseases and their Treatment: with an Essay on Parturition in the Cow. By J. R. DOBSON. Crown 8vo. with Illustrations. 7s. 6d.

Works of Utility and General Information.

The THEORY and PRACTICE of BANKING. By H. D. MACLEOD, M.A. Barrister-at-Law. Second Edition, entirely remodelled. 2 vols. 8vo. 30s.

A DICTIONARY, Practical, Theoretical, and Historical, of Commerce and Commercial Navigation. By J. R. M'CULLOCH. New and thoroughly revised Edition. 8vo. price 63s. cloth, or 70s. half-bd. in russia.

The LAW of NATIONS Considered as Independent Political Communities. By Sir Travers Twiss, D.C.L. 2 vols. 8vo. 30s.; or separately, Part I. Peace, 12s. Part II. War, 18s.

The CABINET LAWYER; a Popular Digest of the Laws of England, Civil, Criminal, and Constitutional: intended for Practical Use and General Information. Twenty-third Edition. Fcp. 8vo. price 7s. 6d.

PEWTNER'S COMPREHENSIVE SPECIFIER; A Guide to the Practical Specification of every kind of Building-Artificers' Work; with Forms of Building Conditions and Agreements, an Appendix, Foot-Notes, and a copious Index. Edited by W. Young, Architect. Crown 8vo. price 6s.

The LAW RELATING to BENEFIT BUILDING SOCIETIES; with Practical Observations on the Act and all the Cases decided thereon; also a Form of Rules and Forms of Mortgages. By W. Tidd Pratt, Barrister. Second Edition. Fcp. 3s. 6d.

COLLIERIES and COLLIERS: A Handbook of the Law and Leading Cases relating thereto. By J. C. Fowler, of the Inner Temple, Barrister. Second Edition. Fcp. 8vo. 7s. 6d.

The MATERNAL MANAGEMENT of CHILDREN in HEALTH and Disease. By Thomas Bull, M.D. Fcp. 5s.

HINTS to MOTHERS on the MANAGEMENT of their HEALTH during the Period of Pregnancy and in the Lying-in Room. By the late Thomas Bull, M.D. Fcp. 5s.

HOW to NURSE SICK CHILDREN; containing Directions which may be found of service to all who have charge of the Young. By Charles West, M.D. Second Edition. Fcp. 8vo. 1s. 6d.

NOTES on LYING-IN INSTITUTIONS; with a Proposal for Organising an Institution for Training Midwives and Midwifery Nurses. By Florence Nightingale. With several Illustrations. 8vo. price 7s. 6d.

NOTES on HOSPITALS. By Florence Nightingale. Third Edition, enlarged; with 13 Plans. Post 4to. 18s.

CHESS OPENINGS. By F. W. Longman, Balliol College, Oxford. Fcp. 8vo. 2s. 6d.

A PRACTICAL TREATISE on BREWING; with Formulæ for Public Brewers, and Instructions for Private Families. By W. Black. 8vo. 10s. 6d.

MODERN COOKERY for PRIVATE FAMILIES, reduced to a System of Easy Practice in a Series of carefully-tested Receipts. By Eliza Acton. Newly revised and enlarged Edition; with 8 Plates of Figures and 150 Woodcuts. Fcp. 6s.

WILLICH'S POPULAR TABLES, for ascertaining, according to the Carlisle Table of Mortality, the value of Lifehold, Leasehold, and Church Property. Renewal Fines, Reversions, &c. Seventh Edition, edited by Montague Marriott, Barrister-at-Law. Post 8vo. price 10s.

MAUNDER'S TREASURY of KNOWLEDGE and LIBRARY of Reference: comprising an English Dictionary and Grammar, Universal Gazetteer, Classical Dictionary, Chronology, Law Dictionary, a Synopsis of the Peerage, useful Tables, &c. Revised Edition. Fcp. 8vo. price 6s.

INDEX.

Spottiswoode & Co., Printers, New-street Square, London.